## A shot from the trees punched the assassin to the ground

Mack Bolan centered his own weapon on the space between her eyes and held his ground. "It's over."

"The hell it is." A scarlet grin twisted her lips.

"Pack it in," he said calmly, "and you still get to live."

"No way, buddy. I'm not your ordinary kind of guy. I get to live anyway."

Her voice held a curious cadence and intonation that the Executioner couldn't place. He glanced at her injuries. "You're in no shape to walk out of here."

Her black eyes had a sheen of madness. "I'm not going to walk out of here, I'm going to fly." She laughed. "Kill me now, and I just come back. The Wild Hunt continues." In one fluid movement she placed the pistol against her temple and pulled the trigger, the force of the blast throwing her head to one side.

# MACK BOLAN ®

## The Executioner

# DON PENDLETON'S
# THE EXECUTIONER®
## SELECT FIRE

THE ARMS TRILOGY

★ BOOK I ★

## A GOLD EAGLE BOOK FROM
# WORLDWIDE®

TORONTO • NEW YORK • LONDON
AMSTERDAM • PARIS • SYDNEY • HAMBURG
STOCKHOLM • ATHENS • TOKYO • MILAN
MADRID • WARSAW • BUDAPEST • AUCKLAND

First edition March 1995
ISBN 0-373-61195-1

Special thanks and acknowledgment to
Mel Odom for his contribution to this work.

SELECT FIRE

Printed in U.S.A.

...the right of the people to keep and bear arms, shall not be infringed.

—Constitution of the United States
Second Amendment, 1791

The most solid moral qualities melt away under the effect of modern arms.

—Ferdinand Foch,
Precepts, 1919

It is a basic right for Americans to bear arms, and I have no quarrel with the Constitution. But arms merchants willing to break people's backs for the sake of making a dollar are fair game for the Executioner's cleansing flame.

—Mack Bolan

# THE
# MACK BOLAN®
## LEGEND

Nothing less than a war could have fashioned the destiny of the man called Mack Bolan. Bolan earned the Executioner title in the jungle hell of Vietnam.

But this soldier also wore another name—Sergeant Mercy. He was so tagged because of the compassion he showed to wounded comrades-in-arms and Vietnamese civilians.

Mack Bolan's second tour of duty ended prematurely when he was given emergency leave to return home and bury his family, victims of the Mob. Then he declared a one-man war against the Mafia.

He confronted the Families head-on from coast to coast, and soon a hope of victory began to appear. But Bolan had broken society's every rule. That same society started gunning for this elusive warrior—to no avail.

So Bolan was offered amnesty to work within the system against terrorism. This time, as an employee of Uncle Sam, Bolan became Colonel John Phoenix. With a command center at Stony Man Farm in Virginia, he and his new allies—Able Team and Phoenix Force—waged relentless war on a new adversary: the KGB.

But when his one true love, April Rose, died at the hands of the Soviet terror machine, Bolan severed all ties with Establishment authority.

Now, after a lengthy lone-wolf struggle and much soul-searching, the Executioner has agreed to enter an "arm's-length" alliance with his government once more, reserving the right to pursue personal missions in his Everlasting War.

# PROLOGUE

*Monaco, 1987*

Though almost two years removed from her beat-cop life-style, and more than an ocean away from her old stomping grounds in Seattle, Washington, Giselle Harte's inner warning alarm went off and pumped adrenaline into her nervous system. She paused outside her hotel, listening to the rain tapping against her umbrella.

*"Mademoiselle?"* the cabdriver said to draw her attention, poking his head out the window. Moisture clung to the peaked edges of his cap. He said something in French, too quick for Harte to catch.

"A moment," she replied in English.

"Of course." The cabbie touched the brim of his hat and ducked back inside.

The street was narrow and dark, part of Monaco-Ville, the oldest section of the country. Traffic was sparse. It was after eight p.m., well into the festive hours of the nightly carnivals that drew the rich and famous from all over the world. The rain was gentle and welcome, cutting into the unaccustomed heat that had baked into the principality most of the day.

Nothing appeared to be amiss, but this wasn't the back alleys of Seattle Harte had come to know and fear, and dangers here could easily go unrecognized.

*"Mademoiselle."*

Irritably Harte opened the cab door and clambered inside. She caught the driver staring at the expanse of leg allowed by the slitted dress she wore and met his gaze with a frank intensity meant to put him in his place.

"You're alone?" he asked.

"But not helpless," she responded coolly.

The man grinned with embarrassment. "Of course. Your destination?"

Harte shook the rain from her folded umbrella and closed the door, then gave the address of the casino at Monte Carlo from memory. She glanced back down the street. Nothing was there.

Chiding herself for coming down with a case of the nerves, she reached into her purse, took out a cigarette and lighted it.

"What brings you to Monaco?" the cabbie asked in accented English.

"Vacation," Harte replied. Beyond the soccer field not far from her hotel, the black and slippery surface of the sea collided with the cottony charcoal of the cloudy sky. The country was small, the second-smallest independent state in the world after Vatican City, according to the hotel's brochures, and bounded on three sides by France. Except for short excursions into British Columbia during her college years, and the recent bodyguard assignments to Vancouver for the migrating Hollywood trade, Harte had never been outside the continental United States. The whole experience still held a quality of unreality about it—except for the sensation of being watched that had swept over her in the hotel lobby.

"You're American?"

"Yes."

"Lots of Americans here this time of year."

"Really." A few minutes later the taxi entered Monte Carlo. Harte glanced at the shady little squares and narrow passageways that really didn't qualify as alleys in her way of thinking. At this time of day Monte Carlo was busy, inhabited by people from all over the world. Some were chronic gamblers who lived with the belief that they had a system to beat the odds. Others were curious onlookers who came to gawk at the famous and wealthy. Yet others were predators, looking for an easy mark. The thought left Giselle Harte cold. She dropped her hand into her purse and took out the small can of hairspray she carried there. It wasn't pepper spray, but coupled with the lighter she still held in her other hand, the spray would be a potent weapon if necessary.

"*Oui.* I've had two other fares from that hotel tonight and taken them to the casino. You should have just gone together and saved a few francs."

"They were Americans too?"

"*Oui.*"

Harte dismissed the questions that came to mind. She couldn't really look a gift horse in the mouth. She'd won the vacation after her agency, Chesterson Security, had entered her name. She'd never won anything in her life, and after the sting operation Internal Affairs had engineered to take down her vice partner, she hadn't really hesitated about going. Especially after her superior had cleared her schedule and given his blessings. She exhaled smoke and tried to put the past out of her mind. It had been a raw deal. Durant had been dirty and she'd had her suspicions, but IA hadn't hesitated about breaking her badge as well as her partner's during the sting. Eleven years with the Seattle PD had gone down the tubes in a single evening, and she'd never taken a payoff. Even Durant's testimony hadn't saved her.

The cab glided to a stop in front of a building whose facade was ornately carved wood. The driver leaned over the seat and quoted the price.

Harte counted out the amount and added a ten-percent tip as she scanned the casino. As she reached for the door, a man stepped out of the darkness and opened it for her.

"Your name please? I am to escort you to your meeting area. We will not be going to the main gambling section of the casino." The man was dressed in a dark suit that looked blue black in the night. His chin held a dusting of blue from a five-o'clock shadow.

Harte was schooled enough to notice the jacket had been cut to conceal a shoulder rig. She got out and moved without stopping so her back wouldn't be against the open door of the cab.

"Giselle Harte."

The man gave her a brief smile. "This way, please, Miss Harte." He offered his arm.

She took it and watched the cab fade into the falling rain. Still, the persistent feeling wouldn't leave her that something predatory was lurking in the night. At the short flight of stairs leading up into the casino, she turned to rake her gaze across the staggered line of buildings across the street.

To the left, near the shortwave radio antenna that resembled a cross, something glassy or metallic glinted for just an instant.

"Miss Harte," her escort prompted.

She looked back at him, aware that another cab had pulled to a stop at the curb. She dismissed the feeling, telling herself she was here for a much-needed vacation and not to waltz with shadows. Monaco had a police force. She thanked the man, then headed into the casino.

"GISELLE HARTE."

Alexander De Moray trained his night-vision binoculars on the woman stepping into the casino. "She's the one from Seattle."

"Yes, sir," his second replied.

Interest flared in De Moray. The woman was much more attractive than he'd figured, and she was one of the top targets for tonight's exercise. Most of the females in that category looked hard and worn. He shifted under the poncho, testing the weight of the Uzi hanging from a shoulder sling and the Colt .45 leathered on his right hip. Built tall and rangy, with shoulders muscled from tending fishing nets in his native New Orleans during his youth, De Moray was an intense man. His eyes burned black in the darkness, and his hair fell across his brow in waves of curly black.

"And there's Weldon York."

"That's the lot of them," De Moray said.

"Yes, sir."

"Then let's get at it." He took the lead, crossing the rooftop and sliding down the metal fire escape. Aware of his second calling out orders, he marked the drifting shapes falling into the positions he'd assigned them. They worked like the fingers of a very deadly hand as they closed in on the casino, brandishing automatic weapons.

"WINE?" the liveried waiter asked.

"Please," Harte answered. "The white." He poured a generous glass and she accepted it, immediately wandering around the fringes of the group collected in a wing off the main gambling area of the casino. At least forty people were gathered in the great hall that was decked out in long purple curtains and gold trim. The inside was chill and made Harte think about the interior of an old medieval castle. Only in this one, the sconces were fueled by electricity, gleaming brightly in brass-and-glass depths.

She eavesdropped with casual abandon. Curiously most of the party's attendees were American, and they were involved in the security industry. She'd learned that from the snatches of conversation she'd overheard.

A buffet had been set up at one side of the room, leaving a portion of the waxed tile floor open for dancing. Staff circulated within the group easily, offering fresh drinks and appetizers. She noticed there weren't many women among them, except for a dozen or so that might have passed as models, especially in the evening gowns they wore.

She cruised through the buffet line and took a small plate, efficiently assembling a croissant sandwich of ham and cheese. Finding a corner near a brocaded drape decorated with rearing wheat-colored lions, she settled in to watch, wondering how soon she could leave without offending the host.

A short man with thick shoulders and a receding hairline stopped in front of her and smiled. He carried a beer stein full of bubbly amber and a small plate of steamed vegetables. "Is this corner taken?"

"Not all of it," Harte responded.

"Do you mind?"

"No."

"Mike Ryerson," the man said, balancing his load so he could offer his hand.

Harte gave him her name and her hand.

Ryerson fell in naturally beside her and watched the crowd, as well. "You a PI?"

She looked at him, but he didn't look back. "I work for Chesterson Security."

"Back in the States?"

"Yes."

"Cop?"

"Once."

Ryerson gave a dry laugh. "So was I. Been independent for six years now." He regarded her with frank brown eyes. "A lot of ex-cops and security people here."

"I noticed."

"Figured you had. Makes you wonder if we're the only suspicious people in this little gathering."

"You won a free trip, too."

"Yeah. My secretary answered an invitation I would normally have put in the circular file. But she thought I needed a trip. I think she was as surprised as I was.

Since my divorce, she's been trying to kick me back into social circles."

More people had started to drift onto the dance floor as the wine and alcohol loosened them up. Dead silence sounded for just an instant, then the hidden speakers kicked loose again at a higher decibel range, unleashing a raucous rock number. The atmosphere became immediately festive.

"You feel like sticking around for this?" Ryerson asked.

"No."

"Me, neither. I saw you over here and you looked as uneasy as I felt, and I was thinking if we talked for a bit, then left together—"

"That we wouldn't draw as much attention if we acted like a couple interested in our own amusement."

Ryerson smiled at her. "Right. When I get these weird feelings, I pay attention to them. Kept my ass intact while I was working homicide in Indianapolis."

Harte ditched the wineglass and plate on a small table nearby. "I'm ready." Ryerson took her by the elbow and guided her toward the entrance. Before they made the threshold, a man dressed in a rain-drenched black poncho swung into her path and blocked her. He held a pistol in his fist, and the huge barrel was targeted directly on her face.

"Leaving so soon?" the man asked in a quiet, deadly voice. His tone was sardonic. "The party's hardly started yet."

Harte had a brief impression of Ryerson moving at her side, then the dark man's gun jumped like a rattler uncoiling and spit a single booming round. The heavy slug caught Ryerson in the face and threw him backward.

Pushed by panic, she tried to run, but the dark man locked his fingers in her hair and dragged her in front of him. He trained the pistol on her left eye. "Don't," he growled. "I don't want to see you dead, but I will if you give me no choice."

As if in response to his shot, the large and elegant windows of the casino came apart in a blinding hail of autofire. Bullets thunked into flesh as well as walls, and the people on the dance floor went down like wheat before a threshing machine.

Black-clad wraiths came in through every door and window, moving mercilessly among the unarmed people. Smoke and explosive grenades added to the confusion and the death toll.

A frozen part of Harte's mind, trained by the horrors she'd seen in her own career, took stock of the unfolding events. One of the dance girls was shot three times at point-blank range and fell onto one of the buffet tables, where her dress caught fire from the small brazier in use to make crepes. Another man, wearing glasses, ran toward her, then his head came apart, shattered by a bullet.

Harte heard herself moaning. The man holding her systematically killed two other men, taking time to confirm his victims. A cruel smile twisted his lips when he looked at her, his magnetic black eyes blazing.

Unwilling to give up and die so easily, Harte raked out at his face with a handful of nails. He avoided her easily, yanking her head back by the hair and throwing himself bodily on top of her to trap her flailing arms. His voice was soft and Southern when he spoke, and his words carried above the din of gunfire.

"Remember me, little darling, because you and I are one. You'll find me in yourself the next time you look." Then he leaned forward and kissed her. She tried to bite him, but he was too fast, and there was the sensation of a needle being slid into the flesh of her right elbow. She struggled helplessly. "Welcome to the Wild Hunt."

The drug blossomed inside her, filled her, numbed her and swept away her senses. The last thing she could remember was the haunting smile on the dark man's face.

**1**

Mack Bolan sensed the death web wound about the bed-and-breakfast before he saw any indication of it. The cool air drifting in from the English Channel made his breath plume before him, and the breeze ripped it away.

He was ten minutes early for the meet. A glance at the two men in the five-year-old British sedan across the street told him they'd been there for some time. One of them was smoking, and the low rumble of their voices carried onto the street. Leaning up against a telephone pole farther on, a third man kept watch over the alley adjacent to the bed-and-breakfast house.

The warrior wondered if the contact man arranged by Stony Man Farm was still inside the building. Then he put the question out of his mind because there was only one way to know for sure.

He jogged down the street and turned right, scanning the area and finding no one. He cut down the alley that led back to the bed-and-breakfast. Gravel crunched underfoot until he got off the rock-covered pathway and became part of the shadows clinging to the small backyards behind the line of houses.

He went quietly, easily picking out the target he sought. Two men were on guard in the darkness, both of them outside the low stone wall that surrounded the bed-and-breakfast's yard. Thirty yards separated them, and they were doing a good job of staying out of sight.

Like a big jungle cat, the Executioner closed on the nearer man, coming up on the guy before he even knew the warrior was there. "Hey," Bolan said in a graveyard whisper that carried no farther than the man's ears.

The guy came around, his hand digging in his jacket pocket with deadly intent.

Before the man could clear his weapon, the Executioner smashed him in the face with a roundhouse elbow to the jaw that left his victim senseless. Quietly Bolan stretched him out in the shadows beside the low wall. He ran his hands through the guy's clothing and came up with a wallet and a .38 Police Positive with an extra speed-loader. There was no badge in the wallet, so Bolan kept the revolver in his fist as he closed on the other man.

Hunkered low, he crept along the stone wall toward the next target. Acrid smoke from the guy's cigarette reached the warrior's nostrils. Clothed in black, his head covered by a dark blue watch cap, the second man was lean and angular. He was staring intently at the curtained windows of the bed-and-breakfast.

Bolan laid the barrel of his weapon just behind the man's ear and pressed it forward meaningfully. "Freeze."

There was an instant of hesitation, then the man said, "You got it, mate. Just go lightly here."

"You got a weapon?" Bolan asked. He kept the .38's barrel pressed into the hollow between the man's jaw and neck, where it couldn't easily be dislodged by a sudden movement if the guy felt inclined.

"Pistol," the man replied.

"Where?"

"Waistband of my pants. On the left."

Bolan quickly relieved the man of a Browning .380 automatic. "What else?"

"A kosh. Strapped to my right leg."

It was heavy and filled with lead shot. Bolan dropped it into a pocket of the pea coat. The man's accent was British, surprising him somewhat because the only resistance he'd been expecting during the mission was from the IRA. "That had better be all."

"It is. Swear to God, mister."

"On your knees." Once the man was down, Bolan unlaced the guy's work boots and used the laces to bind him. A handkerchief formed a suitable gag. Leaving the man where he'd found him, the warrior vaulted the stone wall effortlessly and crossed the intervening distance to the back of the bed-and-breakfast.

Built more than two hundred years earlier, the hostel was generous with ledges and crannies that he could wedge his gloved fingers and shoes onto. He climbed the distance to the second floor, first window at the corner, and clung there as he stared through the misty chiffon into the room.

Barbara Price, mission controller for the covert operations run by Stony Man Farm from its base in the Blue Ridge Mountains of Virginia, had included a picture of Cale Roby in the package of Intel she'd faxed to the big warrior during his stopover in Calais, France. Details about the mission had been sparing, mentioning only the fact that the Irish Republican Army was involved with an attempt to assassinate England's prime minister during peace negotiations with the terrorist group near Dover.

Roby was short, stocky and dark. He sat at a small rolltop desk, gazing anxiously at a clock on a nightstand beside the full-size bed. The sheets and blankets were haphazardly strewed across the bed, giving the impression that Roby had been there for some time. Now he was dressed in gray slacks, a white oxford shirt with an unfurled tie and a deep purple sweater.

The room was furnished in antiques, centered around a four-poster. Doilies covered the nightstand and arms of the armchair. Roses in pastel peach and orange adorned the wallpaper between lines of green.

Bolan rapped his knuckles against the glass, and Roby got up from the chair, almost hiding the small, flat pistol in his hand behind his leg. He pulled the chiffon curtains to one side and gazed at the Executioner.

The warrior gave the password. "Hammett."

"Christie," Roby said, responding with the countersign. He unlatched and lifted the window. "You're Belasko?"

Bolan nodded and clambered through the window.

"We've got company," Roby said. "I'm surprised you weren't accosted."

"I was busy doing the accosting," the warrior replied dryly. "Outside the backyard there are two men I had to neutralize to make this meet."

"Dead?"

"No." It wasn't the Executioner's way to make war on innocents, and for now he didn't know who the men were. "But we're working on borrowed time here. Do you have the package?"

"Sure. I'm pretty certain they tossed my room while I stepped out for my supper. I'd noticed them earlier, so I gave them plenty of time and went early. They were thorough and neat, but they didn't find my cache." Roby crossed the room to the bedside and produced a pocketknife. "Old houses like this, they usually left some space between the walls. Skilled use of a glue stick, a little patience and a small ripsaw smuggled in under Mrs. Arbogast's energetic snooping, and I had a hiding place that suited my needs." He peeled the wallpaper off, then flicked the thin knife blade between freshly sawed boards to free them. Laying the short boards aside, he reached into the wall and extracted a small backpack.

After pulling the curtain, Bolan took the backpack and headed for the bathroom. A claw-foot bathtub dominated the room amid a clutter of toiletries that would have outfitted a small family.

"Mrs. Arbogast," Roby explained with a shrug. "Cleanliness is next to godliness."

The warrior sat on the edge of the tub and opened the backpack. Inside was a series of faxed sheets and eight-by-ten photographs. A brief examination didn't turn up any one subject, though several of the faces were shown again and again in different settings that suggested other countries. He looked up at Roby. "My contact said you could brief me on the parameters of this mission."

Producing a battered gray metal cigarette case, Roby plucked one out and ignited it. He spoke through the cloud of gray smoke he breathed out. "Have you heard of the Huntsman?"

Bolan nodded. "An assassin for hire. Predominantly does work in Europe and the Middle East."

"Correct. Your contact got wind of the fact that the Huntsman's current obligation involves killing the prime minister during the latest series of talks with the IRA. The operative theory for the moment is that the Sinn Fein hired him."

Fanning the pictures, Bolan asked, "Which one is he?"

"That's the rub, I'm afraid." Roby offered a rueful grin. "Nobody knows who the Huntsman is. Or even if he's a he or she's a she. The only thing that really stands out in the Huntsman's career is the fact that the success rate is extremely intimidating. As far as our intelligence was able to ascertain, a target has never been missed during the past six years—even after the Huntsman was reportedly killed in some of the actions."

Bolan scanned the pictures again. The selections seemed to include both sexes, at least half a dozen nationalities, and an age group ranging from late twenties to early sixties. He shoved the pictures and text into the backpack and zipped it closed. "I was also told you could provide a secure phone."

"Not here."

"Understood." Roby wasn't really the man's name. From Price's conversation, the guy was part of the British intelligence community that the CIA had access to for joint ventures. The mission controller had finessed borrowing him to do courier work on the

United Kingdom leg of the mission. "We're wasting time here."

The Briton nodded and led the way from the bathroom.

"When is the attempt supposed to go down?" the warrior asked as Roby gathered his jacket from the bed.

"Tonight. There's a banquet at Yellowfox Farm off A258 on the way to Deal. The PM is supposed to have a late dinner with some of the IRA chaps to kick off the talks."

"Any idea who put out the contract?"

"Among the Sinn Fein? No."

"Then why is the prime minister the target?" Bolan asked. "Taking down any of the peace-talk participants would generate the necessary confusion to break it off."

"Right. Interesting, yes?"

Before Bolan could reply, his hearing warned him of the light footfalls outside the bedroom door. They were too measured and cautious to belong to someone who was simply approaching the room on legitimate business. Reflexes took over and he reached out for Roby, grabbing the man by his arm and yanking him back.

Hoarse whispers were drowned out by the bullets that smashed through the oak door.

"Bloody hell!" Roby roared as he dodged to one side.

Bolan tried for the .38 in the pocket of the pea coat but wasn't able to free it before the door crashed open, propelled by a big man wielding a pistol. The muzzle bounced uncertainly for a moment, then centered on the warrior's chest.

Instantly in motion, the Executioner struck with the backpack. The documents inside gave it enough weight to whirl the straps around the man's wrist twice. Yanking back on the backpack, Bolan pulled the gunner off balance and lifted a knee into the man's groin. A round sizzled by the warrior's cheek and ripped a scar along the flowered wallpaper. Before the man could bring the gun around, the Executioner had the .38 in his hand. He aimed point-blank at the man's head and squeezed the trigger twice. He released the dead man and stepped away.

"There'll be another one," the warrior said to Roby.

The man gave a tight nod and held his own weapon in both hands, covering the door.

Looping the straps of the backpack over one arm, Bolan crossed the room to the window while Roby helped himself to the fallen man's pistol. He swept his eyes across the backyard, barely glimpsing the sudden movement almost flush with the old house.

Bullets crashed through the panes, scattering glass shards and broken bits of latticework across the room. With a whirl of chiffon, the curtains ripped from the window and floated to the hardwood floor.

"The front door," Bolan said, moving in that direction.

Roby nodded and followed.

Part of the warrior's mind was already busy sorting through the details of how the team had run him to ground. It was obvious they were waiting for him.

He paused at the doorway for just an instant, recognizing by the wave of screams in the hallway that the other gunner inside the premises was still on the move. Readying the .38 Police Positive, he whirled.

A railing festooned with artificial flowers ran the length of the hallway to the narrow stairs that led to the parlor on the main floor. Suspended by black chain, an ornate light fixture hung from the ceiling over the open space, casting a dim light over the interior of the house.

The other gunner was backing away, his hands knotted around a Sterling Mark 6 submachine gun. Seeing Bolan, he raised his weapon and unleashed a burst that ripped a pair of landscape paintings from the wall. The 9 mm rounds made an uneven line as they closed on the door.

Easing back the hammer on the .38, the Executioner made his shot deliberate. At the moment, ammo wasn't a luxury. He took up the trigger slack and felt the pistol jump in his fist.

The .38 bullet smashed into the gunman's upper right chest and knocked him off balance. Before he could recover, Bolan thumbed back the hammer and put the next round between his eyes. Listing wildly, the corpse lost its footing and plummeted down the staircase.

The warrior raced to the stairs and vaulted down, landing hard. The main doorway opened in the foyer, and a trench-coated figure tried to step inside. Any confusion about whose side he was on evaporated when he lowered a 12-gauge shotgun into position and cut loose. A small table holding a decorative bowl and pitcher at the bottom of the stairs to Bolan's left shattered as the double-aught buckshot blew it apart.

Still on the move, the Executioner triggered the remaining three rounds in the .38. All of the bullets were on target, roughly shoving the gunner backward. Dumping the .38 into a coat pocket, Bolan dropped to one knee and fisted the Sterling machine gun. A quick frisk of the dead man who'd tumbled down the stairs turned up an extra magazine. Moving to the door, he ejected the partially spent clip from the Sterling and shoved the fresh one home. Less than ten rounds remained in the used magazine. His hand found the light switch and snapped it off.

"Have you got a car?" he asked Roby as the Briton moved into position by the door beside him.

"No. Didn't want to be traceable, so I used the public transport."

Bolan had done the same, coming in by Hovercraft from Calais, then by bus and by foot. He glanced out the nearest window and down the street to where he'd seen a dump truck parked against the curb earlier. The vehicle was still there, almost a hundred yards away, and bearing a full load of crushed rock.

The sedan he'd spotted earlier was squared off and sitting in the middle of the street, facing in the opposite direction from the dump truck. Its lights were flared out over the street.

"Do you know how to hot-wire an ignition?" Bolan asked.

"Yes."

At the top of the stairs, an older lady with blue hair and pink curlers was shrilling questions in Roby's general direction. Despite the gunfire, the woman carried on with admirable regality.

"Mrs. Arbogast," Roby admitted ruefully.

Bolan pointed. "We're going to try for the truck."

Roby glanced in the indicated direction. There was a lull in the gunfire. "Never tried to make an escape in a dump truck before."

"We're not going to make an escape. We're just going to buy some running room."

Producing a small penknife, Roby nodded. "You say go, mate, and we're off."

Cradling the Sterling, Bolan said, "I make my move, you give me a three-count, then streak for the truck."

"And if you're not there when I get there?"

"Leave without me and get in touch with my people. Let them know what happened."

"Luck, then."

"Same to you." Bolan took a last glance around, knowing the shadows moving out in the front yard were the killers closing the deadly net that had been strung around the bed-and-breakfast. Grabbing the curtain partially obscuring the large latticework window overlooking the east side of the house, the warrior covered his face for protection, then flung himself through the glass.

The sounds of the shattering panes were quickly drowned out by the gunfire that surrounded him. He kept his feet under him as he ripped the curtain away.

A figure loomed before him as the countdown for Roby's break started in his head. Bolan swept the Sterling up and tugged on the trigger, unleashing a 3-round burst that cut down the gunner in front of him. Without breaking stride, he vaulted the tumbling corpse, took shelter among the trees and scanned the war zone.

He ignored the sedan. For the moment, the people inside the car were the least of his worries. Positioning two more gunners in his mind, he vectored in on them as Roby's three-count came to an end.

He swept a pair of short bursts toward the points he'd identified and drove the men under cover. Evading the return fire, he moved out to take up a new position, staying within the protective foliage as much as possible.

One of the men broke cover to the Executioner's right. The warrior whirled and brought the Sterling to bear. The little subgun chattered out death and knocked the man down. A glance over the warrior's shoulder showed him that Roby was making good use of the diversion.

Someone in the sedan spotted the Briton and shouted orders. The transmission engaged, and it started to roll forward.

A quick look at Roby told Bolan the man had made the dump truck's door. The Executioner pushed himself into an all-out run, dodging through the tangle of bushes and trees. Though he knew he probably wouldn't be able to cause any mortal damage, he fired the rest of the Sterling's clip into the sedan's bodywork.

Bullet holes puckered the side of the vehicle, and sparks jumped from the sheet metal. The men inside ducked and stayed low, and the driver swerved to the side of the street.

Taking advantage of the respite, Bolan sprinted for all he was worth, flying across the shrub-covered ground. For a moment the confusion about which target they were after halted the gunfire. Bolan's hand was on the left-side door handle when the dump truck's engine shivered to life with a throaty roar and the back glass shattered from a bullet's impact. The warrior pulled himself into the passenger seat, then shucked the Sterling's empty clip and slid the partial one home.

"Go!" he shouted to Roby.

The man nodded, then engaged the truck's transmission with a grinding of gears. The dump truck lumbered forward. Burdened by the cumbersome load of broken rock, the vehicle swayed from side to side.

A shot ripped away Bolan's side mirror. Opening the door, he stepped onto the running board and leveled the Sterling. He fired on single-shot, aiming for the front of the pursuing sedan. Bright cracks, fired by the moonlight, appeared in the car's windshield. The driver took evasive action and dropped back for just a moment before putting his foot down harder on the accelerator. It closed the distance easily.

Behind the sedan, a staggered line of men came into view.

The truck struggled, the engine sounding like a bellows pump, and grudgingly gained speed. There was no way it was going to outrun the sedan.

When the Sterling cycled dry, Bolan tossed it away and slipped the .38 and the speed-loader from his pocket. He slipped the extra cartridges into the cylinder with a practiced twist.

"Where are they?" Roby demanded. "I lost them."

"Coming up hard on the right," Bolan responded. A gunner hung out the passenger door of the sedan and unleashed a fully automatic weapon that spit bullets into the dump truck's wooden sideboards.

Sighting carefully, keeping both eyes open as he leveled the .38 in front of him, Bolan squeezed the trigger. The revolver jerked in his hand. For a moment he thought he'd missed due to the uneven ride of the truck and was readying a follow-up shot. Then the gunner seemed to relax quietly, letting the weapon trickle from his fingers.

Roby took the next corner wildly. For a heartbeat, Bolan thought the truck was going to topple over. The sedan's wheels shrilled as it sped up.

"The next corner," the warrior shouted over the roaring engine. "Which way does it go?"

"Either way you want."

"Left, then, at the last possible minute. Let's see if we can shake them."

"We're definitely not going to outrun them."

Bolan fired two more shots, starring the windshield further, then reached back for the dump truck's bed controls. He tested them and found they'd built up sufficient air pressure to act. "Tell me right before you get there."

A brief instant later, Roby shouted, "Now!"

Yanking on the control lever, Bolan tripped the dump sequence. The rear door of the bed opened as the hydraulics forced the load upward. Broken rock skidded out in a flood, bouncing and skittering across the intersection. The dump truck whined as it shuddered through the tight turn and floated across into the oncoming lane.

Anticipating a quick kill because he could outmaneuver the heavier vehicle, the sedan driver sped up. There was a moment of hesitation when the rock spilled out, and the brake lights flared, then disappeared. By the time he realized what the real danger was, the guy had lost the car on the rock and skidded out of control. Before he could recover, the sedan smashed into the side of a building and stalled out.

Bolan hauled himself into the dump truck's cab. "The first alley you come to, let's lose the truck."

Roby gave a tight nod.

Taking his war book from an inside pocket of the coat, the warrior looked up the area around Yellowfox Farm by the light of a small penlight. From a superficial examination of the region, he wouldn't have a hard time getting into the territory relatively unnoticed. The flip side was that neither would the Huntsman. And the Huntsman had had more time to prepare for the hit.

Turning into an alley, Roby killed the dump truck's engine and they clambered out.

"I'll need weapons," Bolan said tersely as they set out west among the closed shops.

"No problem."

Bolan checked his watch. He was already more than an hour behind the schedule Price had pinned to the mission. He was operating on borrowed time, and some of the people at Yellowfox Farm were probably living on it.

ALMOST TWO HOURS LATER, Bolan was deep within the supposedly protected environs of Yellowfox Farm. Dressed in a combat blacksuit over thermal underwear against the night's chill, he moved like a wraith. His features were masked by camouflage cosmetics.

Yellowfox Farm was a little more than eight hundred yards ahead of him, south by southwest of his present position, going by the compass reckoning he'd taken earlier. Five structures, including the main house that loomed three stories tall, comprised the farm. Two were barns that held riding horses and tack. Two other buildings had been built to house guests. A thousand yards to the west was a campground that held at least two hundred sites, complete with electricity. A conservative estimate put the number of recreational vehicles already parked there at sixty.

Bolan shifted, trying to ease cramped muscles. The biting chill of the wind didn't help. He lifted the night-vision binoculars to his eyes and surveyed the main house again.

For publicity reasons and for the view, the formal dining room had been relocated to the second floor, behind a row of large windows on two sides. Intel from Price, confirmed by Roby's people, had let the warrior know the windows had been replaced with bulletproof glass. It cut down on the chances of a long-range attempt, but didn't rule it out. And the IRA terrorists were a group who liked their bombs and explosives at any rate.

Although there was nothing in the Huntsman's slim file to suggest anything other than a passing proclivity for firearms, Bolan didn't put it past the man to use the IRA's weapon of choice.

Most of the guests staying at Yellowfox Farm had garaged their cars in one of the two barns; however, the majority had taken the complimentary bus in from Dover. But fully a half-dozen limousines were parked in the small space behind the main house. Chauffeurs who had every indication of doubling as bodyguards stood beside the cars, seemingly equally divided between representing the British government and the Irish Republican Army spokesmen. Even at a distance, Bolan could see there was no love lost between the two camps.

It was a powder keg awaiting a spark.

And somewhere out in the darkness, the warrior was sure the Huntsman was lying in wait just as he was.

The Executioner had been in place for little more than forty minutes and had observed the movements of the groups staking out Yellowfox Farm. The British moved through the countryside and immediate strike zones surrounding the house with practiced ease. The IRA teams were less orderly in their sweeps, but more openly brandished their weapons.

It was the third team that held Bolan's attention.

As far as he'd been able to ascertain, none of the third team were within the inner perimeters of the farm. He figured they were there as backup and an exfiltration measure for the Huntsman after the assassination attempt. He'd IDed seven members of the third team so far, but had the feeling there were more lurking about. But even though he'd tagged them, he hadn't been able to guess the Huntsman's location or method of attack from the patterns he'd discerned.

He zoomed in with the night lenses, focusing on the line of windows presented to his view from this side of the main house. A surreptitious glance at his watch showed him that it was almost one o'clock in the morning. As yet, neither the British security guarding the prime minister nor the IRA teams seemed to be aware of the third team. Part of the reason was due to the fact that the third team didn't go for deep penetration, and because their movements were so slow and so cautious. Whomever they were, they were well organized and disciplined.

Bolan shifted again, getting his gear balanced for the move as he put the binoculars away in a chest pack. So far, Stony Man Farm hadn't been able to turn up anything on the IDs of the two men he'd bumped into at the bed-and-breakfast. He was betting both identities were false.

Moving with grace and skill, he set out for the farm. He'd chosen a circuitous route that would keep him undercover for nearly the entire distance. It would also bring him in near contact with four members of the third team.

Roby had been good to his word about the weapons, and they'd picked them up with no trouble. Twin Browning Hi-Powers using subsonic 9 mm rounds and silencers rode on his right hip in a counterterrorist drop holster and in jackass-rigged shoulder leather under his left arm. A limited assortment of fragmentation grenades and Thunderflashes from SAS stores were snugged in pockets of the blacksuit. He carried a Gerber Mark II combat knife strapped to his right calf on the outside of his pant leg. For his long weapon, he carried an L-42 A-1 sniper rifle that was derived from the old Lee-Enfield .303 and chambered in 7.62 mm rounds. Even with the bolt action, the Executioner figured he could make good use of the 10-round magazine when the time came. He carried it upside down across his back by a nylon sling equipped with Uncle Mike quick-disconnect swivels.

Reaching the first contact point of his journey, he slipped a wireless ear-throat headset from an inside pocket of the blacksuit and slid it into place. He flicked it on with a thumb and waited for the static to clear a heartbeat later. Before dropping into the war zone, he'd set up a portable satellite transceiver at the top of one of the hills flanking the farm. If Aaron Kurtzman, Stony Man's cybernetics expert, hadn't been able to secure a tamper-free line, the communications wouldn't have taken place.

Bolan thumbed the transmit button. "Stony Base, this is Stony One. Stony Base, this is Stony One. Over."

Barbara Price's voice came back crystal clear. "Go, Stony One, you have Stony Base. Over."

"I've reached the target zone and I'm moving in. Any luck with reaching the sitting duck?"

"The message was signed, sealed and delivered only a few minutes ago by the Man himself, but the Duck's not going anywhere."

"Why?"

"He believes there's too much at stake tonight to lose on a no-show. If an assassin does pop out of the woodwork, he's thinking maybe the threat will consolidate their interests."

"The Duck's got guts," Bolan said. "You have to give the guy that."

"The Man agreed. Our problem is to keep the Duck alive long enough to reap the harvest of what's being sown here tonight."

"Affirmative."

"The Duck and his people know there's an outsider in the mix, but we couldn't cover you in any way whatsoever. You're running naked on this one, Stony One."

Bolan had already figured as much and had planned his strategy accordingly. He took out the night glasses and scanned the territory again. The nearest man belonging to the unidentified third party was less than two hundred yards away. The man was hunkered near the bole of a tree, almost entirely covered by the tall bush beside him. His black clothing turned him into a two-dimensional shadow, but the barrel of the rifle he carried was long and angular, and didn't fit the curvature of the landscape.

"Has the Bear managed to tie into the communications freqs shared by the teams?" Bolan asked.

"The domestic and import teams, yes, but we're having trouble getting the observation line."

"They're running quiet," the warrior said. Even from that distance, he could see the walkie-talkie setup slung over the man's shoulder.

"That's what we thought," Price agreed. "We did manage to track down three of the men who attacked you earlier."

"How?"

"MI-6 records."

"They weren't native, then?"

"Negative. One was a mercenary from South Africa, and the other two were from Germany."

"They have a shared history?"

"Not that we could turn up. They were out on the market, available to whoever could meet their price."

"Have you got any idea about who met it?"

"Not yet, but we've just started working in that direction. One facet that stood out was that all three men had been fairly active on the international scene up until two and a half, three years ago. Then they faded.''

"Until tonight."

"Right."

"Maybe they found steady employment some-where."

"We're checking into that."

"Any ties to the Huntsman?"

"None."

"From the Intel you sent on the Huntsman, I gather that he's a free agent, not working for any one group."

"That's right." Price sounded troubled. "The problem is, Stony One, that if we believe everything we've dug up on the man, he's a ghost. He's been killed a couple times, only to have his body disappear later. Once he was killed as a woman."

"And they identified her as the Huntsman?"

"As well as could be, under the circumstances."

Bolan pondered that, trying to correlate the infor-mation into the scheme that he saw spread out before him. "Maybe whoever hired the Huntsman to make this hit also hired this other team as backup."

"Maybe. But it doesn't ring true."

Lights flared at the far end of the main road that led to Yellowfox Farm. Bolan trained the night glasses on the checkpoint and watched as a pair of guards walked out and demanded identification. The vehicle was a Volkswagen off-road compact. The warrior couldn't make out the driver, but he could see the front license plate and knew instantly it was a rental. "Can you ac-cess a British rental car for me?"

"We can try."

Bolan read off the numbers and continued to watch the vehicle. A late arrival was certainly suspect. Documents were passed out to the guards, and one of them retreated to the portable building that had been set up to work security.

"Got it," Price called back. "The rental belongs to Annalee MacPherson, a reporter for *Signs of Erin,* an underground newspaper in Northern Ireland." She spelled the woman's name.

"Was she invited?"

"Yes."

"Then why is she just now getting there?"

"She checked in with the British and IRA people earlier to let them know she was having car trouble."

"Can you confirm the time on the car rental?"

Computer keys clacked and Bolan could imagine Kurtzman hunkered over his machine quickly negotiating the necessary information. "Three hours ago."

Bolan consulted his watch. "That would have put her late, but not this late. When did she pick up the car?"

"A little more than two hours ago. Is she alone?"

The warrior raked the interior of the small car with the binoculars again, confirming only one visible silhouette inside. "She appears to be. If that's her. I'm not close enough to be certain it's even a woman."

"The prime minister is supposed to address the IRA representatives in ten minutes. Whatever move the Huntsman has planned, it's going to have to happen soon."

The guard returned the documents to the Volkswagen's driver, then waved the car on.

"MacPherson exists?"

"Affirmative, Stony One. She's been in the journalism field for the past three years, and with the Northern Ireland paper for almost two of them."

"Give me a description." Bolan put the night glasses away and got to his feet, setting out at an easy pace that maintained the stealth and silence imperative to this mission, yet hurried him along his path. Once he had the description Price gave him, he cut out of the active com loop. Stony Man Farm was limited to an observational capacity only on this mission.

Less than two minutes later, he closed on the first of his targets. He drew the Browning Hi-Power from his thigh, thumbed the hammer back and thrust the weapon against the back of the guy's head.

Startled, the man still tried to whip around and bring his weapon into play.

Bolan grabbed the rifle by the barrel and kicked out, catching the man in the chest. With a loud grunt of pain, the gunner fell backward and crashed against the tree. The Executioner fired once, and the 9 mm parabellum round chiseled bark from the tree trunk only inches from the man's cheek. The guy's eyes took in the white scar left by the bullet, then placed his hands on his head.

Reversing the rifle in his hand, Bolan rammed it into the soft, loamy ground, packing the barrel tight. "Now we talk," the warrior said in a graveyard voice.

The man nodded.

"Where's the Huntsman?" Bolan demanded.

"I don't know." His accent marked him as Eastern European.

"You're with him?"

"No."

"What's your assignment here?"

The man shook his head. "Take me in if you want. But I'm not talking."

Aiming with deliberation, Bolan lifted the Hi-Power. "I don't have time to take you in. If you can't help me, you're useless."

A burst of static issued from the man's radio and almost masked the soft footfall that sounded behind Bolan. Reacting with instinctive speed, the warrior leaped to one side as bullets cut through the space he'd just been occupying. He caught himself on one hand and turned the leap into a forward roll, his questing eyes spotting the other gunner almost at once. The man's weapon was silenced, but the muzzle-flashes lighted up the immediate vicinity with yellow-orange undertones.

Before he completed the forward roll, Bolan had targeted the new arrival and squeezed the Browning's trigger four times, whispering sudden death. At least three of the rounds caught the man in the chest and sent him spinning backward. Coming to his feet and seeing his onetime prisoner freeing a handgun from shoulder rigging, he fired two shots from the point. The top of the man's head disappeared and he dropped to the ground.

"Stony One, this is Stony Base. Over."

Bolan checked both the gunners and made sure they were dead. It was a night for surprises, and he was already walking a tightrope between British security and the IRA bodyguards without someone he'd thought safely out of the action coming back on him. "Go, Stony Base. You have Stony One. Over."

"MacPherson never arrived."

Surging to the top of the hill the sniper had been covering, Bolan swept his gaze along the road leading to the farmhouse. "Do the inside security people know?"

"That's affirmative. We're logged into their computer network. They've sent a team out to check on her quietly, without alerting their IRA counterparts."

"If she was forced to bring someone inside the security perimeters, then killed, it could look like a British setup."

"Agreed."

He flicked the binoculars to his eyes and scanned the road. Less than a hundred yards to the east, he found the Volkswagen, almost hidden in brush at the side of the road. Nothing around it moved. A glance at the car pool in front of the farmhouse showed no vehicles in motion. "How are the British teams coming to investigate?"

"On foot. Moving a vehicle was considered too risky."

The decision bought some time, Bolan knew, but it also bought time for the Huntsman. He moved as quickly as he could.

"I've managed to get G-Force into your neck of the woods," Price went on. "He'll be available for exfiltration later, but you'll have to get wet to manage it."

"Roger. How soon is the meet?"

"It's going down now."

Bolan cleared the frequency and pushed himself harder. In little over a minute he'd covered the distance to the Volkswagen.

The car was canted sideways, driven up onto young saplings that hadn't had the strength to support it.

Low-hanging branches from tall trees overhead concealed it from aerial view. Scratches ran the length of the vehicle, signifying that it hadn't gone smoothly.

Following the muzzle of the Browning, Bolan inspected the interior of the car. There was no sign of the woman. The trunk hatch was open, but it was possible that it had sprung during the impact. A quick check with his penlight assured him that nothing significant had been left behind.

His window of covert operations was quickly closing. In the confusion, the Huntsman would be more easily able to track his target. If the IRA and Britons didn't take each other out anyway.

Making his decision, knowing the Huntsman would be relying in part on the undercurrent of tension running through the British security force to create opportunities, Bolan fisted the Gerber combat knife, leaned in under the Volkswagen and punctured the gas tank in three places. The fuel gurgled and spattered out on the ground.

Unlimbering the sniper rifle, he moved away, climbing a steady rise over the area of the wreck that would give him a proper view of the declared war zone. Settling into his chosen spot, he scanned the woods around him, tracking the terrain down to Yellowfox Farm. Two of the snipers were still in position, and he could spot the teams converging on the Volkswagen.

With the numbers counting down in his mind, the warrior ripped a Thunderflash grenade from his pocket, pulled the pin, then lobbed the bomb with unerring accuracy toward the rear of the Volkswagen.

Three seconds later, the Thunderflash went off with a blinding spark of light. A heartbeat later, the spilled fuel went off too, issuing an echoing basso rumble that flowed over the valley.

Ignoring the panorama of colors that flared to life over his shoulder, the Executioner leaned into the tree he took cover behind and looked through the cross hairs of his scope. He picked up his first target and caught the man as he was turning to stare in confusion in the direction of the explosion.

Bolan squeezed the trigger and felt the L-42 A-1 buck against his shoulder. He rode out the recoil and worked the bolt, levering a fresh 7.62 mm cartridge into place. A sweep across the target area assured him a follow-up shot wouldn't be necessary.

The second man was harder, having remained behind the rock formation he was using as cover. Bolan put the cross hairs on an exposed portion of the guy's leg and squeezed off the shot. He had time to work the bolt before the first round hit home. The resounding crack of the bullet crossing the intervening six hundred yards hardly had time to reach the man's ears before the Executioner had the killing shot in the air. The man had turned over and sat up, grabbing at his wounded leg, when the next shot caught him in the forehead.

Unable to pick up the third man he'd chosen for his preemptive strike, Bolan darted away from his position. Already return fire was rattling through the leaves and branches above him.

He hadn't found the Huntsman yet, but he'd guaranteed that a lot more people would be beating the bushes for the assassin and that the prime minister and

IRA peace negotiators would know they were under fire. All he had to do was find his quarry and avoid the traps he'd set into motion for the Huntsman. And somehow get out alive.

For a moment, Annalee ... this was her ... the last contract on ... someone in Switzerland who ... could afford to take all of the eight ... Half expected to die... she had heard of it ... world. Knowing that... knew the job, the one who did it, ... and fled into a dark...

Sequestered in the safety of a copse, able to see almost 360 degrees around him, the Huntsman knelt and opened the attaché case he'd retrieved from the trunk of the rented Volkswagen. He took a moment to use a rubber band to bind the long brunette hair back out of his face, cursing the inconvenient disguise he'd been saddled with on this mission.

His hands were small and delicate, and a gold band gleamed on the third finger of his left hand. He ripped it off and threw it into the brush where it disappeared almost immediately. The H&K PSG-1 match-grade sniper rifle housed in foam cutouts inside the attaché case came together in his hands, forming a single deadly weapon from three pieces. The trigger housing slid into place with a delicate click that brought a smile to his face. Then it was drowned out in the explosion that sounded just behind him.

Whirling, he glanced back at where he had left the rental. The only thing he saw was a spiraling fireball that spit orange and gray clouds toward the black sky. Time had passed, he knew, and Annalee MacPherson's lateness would have been noted. But no one should have taken action like that.

For a moment, dormant feelings struggled within him. He felt confusion and helplessness surface inside him, filling the thin cracks of the splintered mind held captive inside his skull. Pain hammered at his temples, bringing threatening memories from the past as he sank to his knees. The woman had been so weak, so afraid.

But he wasn't.

Resolutely he concentrated on his face. Despite the ringing gunfire that sounded around him, he rebuilt his features inside his own mind, focused to the point that it was like looking into a mirror or into video footage of himself. The curling black hair fell rebelliously over his brow, darkening the sardonic smile that twisted his thin lips. He was sure, if he'd wanted to, he could have felt the smooth texture of his face.

His breathing slowed to something approximating normal. When he blinked his eyes, the Huntsman was once more operating at his peak performance.

He grabbed the H&K PSG-1 and forced himself to his feet, an organic machine moving on its agenda. An earpiece from a radio belted at his waist kept him informed of the communications between the Blackbat Unit members. Evidently they'd lost four of the team to an unknown assailant. The Huntsman had no way to talk to them. The only way they would have anything to do with him was if he didn't make it out on his own.

He covered the ground rapidly, reading the deploying lines of British and IRA security staggered before him. Even with the announcement of what was probably a joint threat, the teams were slow to react.

He breathed as he'd been trained for years, remembering the Special Forces drills. Despite the time he'd spent as a reporter waiting for his calls, he'd maintained excellent physical conditioning.

A sweeping flashlight beam off to his right sent him to ground to avoid detection. Two men with automatic weapons passed by within fifteen feet of him. After they'd disappeared into the night, he launched himself forward again. The sounds of the gunfight were spreading. The Blackbat Unit was clearly confused about who was attacking them with such enthusiasm and accuracy. Reports of a lone man dressed in black came from one man, then he wasn't heard from again.

The Huntsman put it to the back of his mind. He had a job to do, and he didn't intend to fail. He never had—even when he'd been killed.

Less than four hundred yards from the main house, he slowed again. Checking the movement of the enemy troops, he aimed himself at the tree he'd chosen for his vantage point for the shot. He slung the rifle over one shoulder, then clambered up the previously placed mat-finished spikes.

Running his hand over the rough bark of the tree, he found the markings that guided him to his sniping position. The same people who'd placed the spikes in the days before had also cleared part of the foliage, leaving a tunnel almost eighteen inches wide. It would help mask his first couple of shots, but if he needed more than that, he was blown anyway. The cleared distance, though, at three hundred yards, translated into an uninterrupted field of fire across the length and breadth of the main house and of the parking area.

He settled into the crotch of the tree, crossed his legs and rested his elbows on his knees. The rifle was a heavy but familiar weight. Shifting slightly, he brought it up, aiming in profile so his elbows and knees maintained the weight. It was a position he could hold for hours if necessary. He uncapped the lenses and kept both eyes open as he began sweeping the windows of the main house, the people on the other side of the bulletproof glass brought into sharp relief.

He started the search for his target. His hand dipped into his pocket briefly and touched the Vietnamese beer bottle cap that had been made into a key ring. He usually kept it within the leather binder so no one else could see it. The bottle cap was a clue to who and what he really was, and where he'd come from. It was material proof that Death could never cage him.

The bulletproof glass didn't figure into his thinking anymore. The H&K was loaded with armor-piercing rounds that would tear through the windows and Kevlar vests alike.

Someone had turned the lights out in the main house, but the night scope he used brought the scene almost up to daylight levels. He had no trouble spotting the people moving around inside. Patient searching cleared the buffet and meeting rooms visible through the thin curtains. He concentrated on the car pool. The British security people would have their orders to get the prime minister out of the area as soon as possible.

A cool breeze washed over the Huntsman as he locked on to the limousine. The door at ground level burst open and security guards dressed in dark clothes and wearing communications headsets established a perimeter, backing off some of the IRA guns. For a moment the Huntsman thought violence was going to spill over the two groups and ruin his chances of a shot. Then, grudgingly, the IRA backed off. Evidently their leaders had chosen another way out of the building.

The Huntsman took up trigger slack expectantly. The image of the bottle cap on his key ring burned brightly in his mind and settled the confusion of emotions that tried to break loose inside him.

The prime minister came out of the main house hunkered low and running. His arms were wrapped around his head defensively. Four bodyguards surrounded him, waving their guns to cover every possible angle of attack as they hustled him to the waiting limousine.

The Huntsman leaned forward in the tree, setting himself for the coming recoil of the shot. He drew his finger back for the kill.

"FREEZE!"

The voice came from behind Mack Bolan. In a heartbeat, the Executioner judged the distance separating him from the man and went into action. A shot passed by inches over his head and shattered a limb from a tree. Before the broken branch had time to hit the ground, the warrior ducked into the tree line. Bullets chewed into the ground and brush after him.

He paused behind a tree long enough to pluck a Thunderflash grenade from his gear, arm it, then toss it back into the clearing where the man had surprised him. He kept his eyes closed until after the blast to preserve his night vision as best he could.

The man in the clearing cursed with real feeling and radioed his position to whichever part of the security teams he was with.

Bolan had figured the man for part of the bodyguard network. Whomever the third team represented, they weren't interested in taking prisoners. He'd witnessed them cutting down the British patrols as well as the IRA groups.

He pushed himself forward again, staying with the high ground as much as possible. Twice he was sure he'd seen the Huntsman breaking cover against the uneven terrain. At the distance, with the brevity of the sightings, he hadn't been sure whether the figure was that of a woman or a slim man. There'd been no mistaking the intent, though. Besides the Executioner, that person had been the only one moving toward Yellowfox Farm.

He carried the sniper rifle in his left hand and one of the Brownings in the other as he ran. Confusion was everywhere around him. A figure, almost masked behind the brush it used as concealment, moved and drew his attention. He swept the Hi-Power toward it, straight ahead of him, never veering from his course because it had gotten too late for finesse. The clothing was dark and bore none of the identifying markings of the British units or the IRA. He squeezed the trigger rapidly, aiming for the center of the gunman. A bullet burned a furrow along his right side just above his pelvis, painful but not debilitating.

The Hi-Power barked five times, sweeping across the gunner and the tree bent like a rainbow behind him. Fresh white scars lined the bark that matched the gunman's chest height. He toppled silently.

Without breaking stride, Bolan vaulted to the top of the leaning tree and propelled himself onward. By rights, the Huntsman should have been withdrawing. But the warrior understood the mentality. Sometimes in his own wars "retreating" to the front line was the only option for survival or success.

Still one hundred fifty yards out from the Huntsman's position, the Executioner saw the man climb a tree on a ridge overlooking Yellowfox Farm but was unable to secure a shot in time. He couldn't really identify the man from the clothing. The hair had been gathered back, but there was something about the way the man moved that tagged the identification for the warrior.

Calculating the angle necessary to fire down onto the main house, Bolan sprinted right to open an angle for himself, the numbers whistling death through his mind. At the optimum end of his estimated time frame, he threw himself prone and pulled the sniper rifle to his shoulder. He swept the scope over the tree, trying to find his target. Branches and tree trunks protected the Huntsman's blind. The spot had evidently been chosen with considerable thought.

The headset crackled. "Stony Base to Stony One. Over."

"Go," Bolan replied.

"They're calling it," Price radioed. "The meeting's over, and they're bringing the prime minister out until this mess can be sorted through properly. The Huntsman?"

"Still viable and still a threat." Bolan spotted the long barrel of the Huntsman's weapon protruding from the tangled growth of the tree. He was grimly aware of the movement going on at the cars flanking the main house. In the open for only seconds at the most, the British prime minister wouldn't stand a chance against the Huntsman's marksmanship. He ignored the sounds of war echoing around him and concentrated on the sniper scope.

"They're in motion now," Price said.

Presented in profile, nothing of the Huntsman was revealed except the bracing hand under the rifle barrel, and the front part of the scope.

Bolan made his decision in a nanosecond. The cross hairs raised up a notch to settle on the scope's outline. He pulled the trigger, hearing the distant roar of the Huntsman's rifle a second later that told him they'd fired at almost the same time.

"He's fired on the prime minister," Price informed him in a tight voice. "We're picking up the radio transmissions now. They think he's been hit. The bullet sheared through the top of the limousine."

Bolan worked the sniper rifle's action and brought the scope back to his eye. The Huntsman and his weapon had disappeared. Something glittered on a lower limb. Focusing on it, the warrior spotted the twisted wreckage of the scope that had been mounted on his adversary's rifle.

An instant later a human figure came bailing out of the tree like a lunging cat.

The Executioner touched off a second round, but knew the minute the stock thudded into his shoulder that he'd missed. The Huntsman had moved too quickly. Before he could find the man, his quarry had disappeared against the backdrop of the broken terrain.

No question remained in Bolan's mind that the assassin would close in to confirm his kill. He pushed himself up and ran, plotting an intersection course along the road the limousine would take getting back to A258. The British security forces would act on standard procedure and get the prime minister out of the immediate area even if he was dead.

The familiar sounds of a helicopter thundered into the night sky, and a searchlight strobed across the darkness covering the forest around Yellowfox Farm.

Adjusting his course to take advantage of the cover offered from aerial pursuit, Bolan put everything into his stride. Perspiration covered him under the blacksuit despite the chill temperatures, and salt stung the wound in his side. He considered tossing the L-42 A-1 because it slowed him, but he had no idea if he might need the long-distance threat the weapon offered. He drew one of the Brownings with his free hand and glanced back at the main house.

The limousine was in motion now, fishtailing wildly on the loose gravel as the driver cut around in a tight 180 to get the nose headed in the right direction. The lights came on as it cleared the small gate leading to the main road.

"Stony One, this is Stony Base. Over."

"Go." Bolan tried to remember the lay of the land around the road. He hadn't had the chance to explore it firsthand because it had been heavily guarded. He knew it was narrow and tight, cloistered by trees. The Huntsman would be able to ambush with ease if he got there in time.

"The prime minister was *not* hit, Stony One," Price said. "There was some confusion. One of the bodyguards took the hit instead. They're in motion now. Get clear of the area and we can try to follow up on the Huntsman later."

"Can't," Bolan said. The road was coming into view now. "The Huntsman hasn't broken off the attack. He's trying an interception play."

"That's suicide."

"Maybe he knows something we don't. I'll get back to you when I can." The warrior cleared the frequency, slowing as he came to the top of a rise because he knew he could easily be skylined.

On the other side of the ridge, one of the unidentified team members was in radio contact with someone in his group. Lean and dark, his face shadowed by a watch cap, he sat with his back against a tree, his assault rifle cradled across his knees. "I say the hell with it," the guy snarled. "I hired on to get the guy out of here if he needed it, not follow some kind of goddamn Audie Murphy charge to hell and back. If he has some kind of death wish, that's his problem, not mine." There was a pause. "Hey, screw recovering his corpse. That's crazy. I'm taking my advance money and calling it even-Steven."

Aware of the time constraints and that the hovering helicopter had covered the sounds of his approach, Bolan stepped out from hiding with the Browning leveled.

Seeing him suddenly appear, the gunman scrambled to bring up his rifle.

Bolan would have preferred a living witness he could have tried to spirit away later. He didn't have that choice. The Hi-Power bounced three times in his hand. All of the bullets bracketed the man's face, shoving him back into the night.

Breathing hard, his face sweat-streaked, the warrior reached the road's edge. To his left, hurling along as fast as the road conditions would permit, the limousine lunged toward the main highway.

Incredibly the Huntsman seemed to appear from nowhere, arcing from the overhanging hillside and landing in the center of the dirt road in a three-point crouch. The tangle of brunette hair pulled back in a quick ponytail snaked down the back of a figure that definitely held feminine curves. Coolly, as if uncaring about the tons of metal bearing down on her, the Huntsman raised the rifle to her shoulder and sighted down the barrel.

The limousine's engine growled louder as the driver accelerated even more.

Bolan knew it was a shot he could make, and he knew the assassin was capable of it, as well. The first round would kill the driver and cause a wreck that might be fatal. If the crash didn't kill the prime minister, a bomb or follow-up rounds would.

The headlights washed over the Huntsman as she stood her ground. The limousine was within sixty feet or less.

Bolan lifted the Browning and fired from the point, adjusting his aim as he ran and staggered down the hillside. Dirt and gravel jumped around the Huntsman, but she ignored him. Then at least two of the Executioner's rounds hit her in the upper thigh as she squeezed the trigger.

The bullet skipped across the top of the limousine, showering sparks in its wake. Then the big car was on top of the woman. There was no time to get off another shot.

Miraculously she wheeled, turning like a matador evading a bull's horns, but wasn't able to completely escape. The heavy bumper caught her a glancing blow and sent her spinning away as it passed.

The ruby taillights of the limousine flared briefly as it negotiated the next turn.

Bolan's night sight was partially disabled by the headlights as they passed. He blinked to clear it and tried to use his peripheral vision. Slinging the rifle over his shoulder, he took a two-handed grip on the Browning and continued moving forward.

The woman was gone.

Still, the warrior knew she couldn't have gotten far. A blood trail slicked across the broken rock creating the foundation for the road. Whether from his bullets or the slamming impact of the car, he didn't know. He crept slowly forward into the darkness, alert to every movement and sound.

Twenty yards into the brush, the Huntsman broke cover. The rifle barrel was pointed directly at Bolan's head. His combat senses warned him a heartbeat before the detonation crashed through the woods. He lunged to one side, knowing he was safely out of the line of fire and returned fire to impair rather than kill.

The 9 mm parabellum round slammed into the Huntsman's shoulder at the same time his mind registered that the rifle bullet had whined off a tree behind him. Already off balance because of her wounds, the bullet caught her in the shoulder and knocked her to the ground.

He moved in at once, the Browning leveled before him. Her face was a pallid oval in the uneven dark. The helicopter was nearer now, and the column of light jetting from its underbelly raked along the twisting road leading from Yellowfox Farm. He knew the security teams would be closing the area off, and any chance at escape was slipping through his fingers with every tick of the clock.

She watched him with eyes that held the frantic light of a trapped animal. Using her uninjured arm, she pulled a small pistol from her back. She didn't try to point it at him.

Bolan centered his own weapon on the space between her eyes and held his ground. "It's over."

"The hell it is." She sniffed, then spit out bloody phlegm. A scarlet grin twisted her lips.

From the description Price had given him, Bolan was certain he was looking at Annalee MacPherson. "Pack it in," he said calmly, "and you still get to live."

"No way, buddy. I'm not your ordinary kind of guy. I get to live anyway."

Her voice held a curious cadence and intonation that the Executioner couldn't place. He glanced at her injuries. In addition to the bullet wounds, her leg had been broken by the impact of the limousine. He didn't see how she'd gotten around as it was. "You're in no shape to walk out of here."

Maniacal laughter exploded from her, turning into a coughing fit that shook her body.

Bolan stared forward, intending to seize her weapon before she could recover.

Instead she waved him back with her wounded arm and jammed the muzzle of her pistol to her own head. Her eyes looked black and held a sheen of madness. "I'm not going to walk out of here, I'm going to fly." She laughed again. "Kill me now, and I just come back. The Wild Hunt continues." She pulled the trigger, and the concussion threw her head to one side.

Even before he reached her, Bolan knew she was dead. His fingers pressed against the flesh of her neck under her jawline, seeking a pulse. None was there. In death, there was something soft and fragile about her, as if some kind of innocence had returned to her.

"Stony Base to Stony One. Over."

"Go." Bolan went through her clothing quickly.

"Break it off," Price advised. "They've got people all over that area searching for you. We'll get another chance at the Huntsman later on."

There was nothing in the pockets of the woman's black clothing except for one reload for the rifle. There were no extra shells for the pistol she'd used to kill herself. Fighting her way to freedom hadn't been a consideration. Whatever ID she presented at the gatehouse had to have been left in the car or thrown out along the way. He glanced back at the region where he'd torched the Volkswagen. The sky still held a soft orange nimbus that told him it was still burning.

"I've got the Huntsman," Bolan radioed back. "Maybe."

"Can you repeat that, Stony One? One of the other frequencies was stepping all over you."

The warrior stood and reworked the nylon sling holding the rifle so it would cross his chest, the barrel pointing down. In the distance, the sporadic gunfire had almost died away. "The backup team I ran into were under orders to take the Huntsman's body out of here if she was terminated."

"She?"

"Yeah. This one was definitely a she. From the description, I'd also say she was Annalee MacPherson. Or someone who looked enough like her to pass as her." Bolan scanned the darkness. From the way a dozen or more lights were swinging back and forth nearly a hundred yards from his position, he figured someone had set up a foot-patrol dragnet through the area.

"You're talking like there's more than one Huntsman," Price said.

"At this point, don't rule it out. Use your contacts to get a message to the prime minister that the Huntsman may still be gunning for him."

"Affirmative."

The big warrior fed a fresh clip into the Browning he'd used to bring the Huntsman down, then holstered it. He didn't intend to confront any of the legitimate security people at Yellowfox Farm, but some of the backup team might still be trying to carry out their exfiltration orders. "I'm going to attempt to make it out of here with the body. If they're willing to go to lengths to try to recover it, maybe it can tell us something."

"That's too much of a risk."

Bolan didn't try to relay his feelings about the innocence he'd seen in the woman's death. His reaction was confusing, and he didn't know where it had come from. "The way I see it, the risk is in letting those people recover the body. Run MacPherson through the Bear's computers again and see if something shakes out when you lean into it. Also, check out references to something called the 'Wild Hunt.' She mentioned it right before she killed herself."

"Understood. You stay hard out there."

"No other way to be," the Executioner replied. He broke the connection, then took one of the empty ammo pouches from his gear and slipped it over the dead woman's face to prevent her complexion from giving him away as he moved. He knelt and draped the deadweight over his shoulder, then moved out as quickly as he could to evade the approaching line of searchers.

**3**

"They found and destroyed the portable satellite transceiver Striker had set up."

Barbara Price looked up from the stuffed manila file folder she'd been studying. "So we've lost him?"

Seated behind the big horseshoe-shaped desk that was the centerpiece of the computer room where he kept his finger on the pulse beat of a world, Aaron Kurtzman grimaced. "'Lost' is kind of a strong word. The last we heard, he was still active."

"And being chased by British security people at Yellowfox Farm."

"True. But they haven't caught him yet. Carmen has logged us into their com net. They can't know anything without us knowing immediately afterward." Although trapped in a wheelchair by an assassin's bullet for years, Kurtzman still deserved his sobriquet of Bear. He looked as though he'd have been more at home hammering out new wagon wheels as a nineteenth-century village smithy than as a cybernetics wizard manning the computer consoles spread out around him.

Price closed the file and set it aside. She'd been going over detail work concerning the events Phoenix Force would soon be enmeshed in during their assignment in Jerusalem. None of the updates had added anything to their present store of knowledge that was going to change events there.

"What about Jack?" she asked.

"He's standing by in Calais in a seaplane, just minutes away from Striker. There was no way to get him into Dover tonight on legitimate business."

Price cleared her mind and concentrated on the various assignments she was marshaling. The Stony Man teams were spread out across the globe, and all were on the point of active engagement. At the same time Bolan worked the investigative foray into Great Britain, Phoenix Force was digging in to manage a holding position during talks between the Israelis and radical Palestinians in Jerusalem, while Able Team was preparing a punitive action against a crew of international gunrunners in Queen Charlotte Sound off the coast of British Columbia.

"You taped the conversation Striker had with the Huntsman?" she asked.

Kurtzman nodded.

"Play it back."

The big man tapped the keyboard in front of him. Seconds later, the woman's pain-filled voice issued from a small speaker in the computer setup, not broadcasting loud enough to be heard more than a few feet from the desk.

The deranged laughter sent icy fishhooks rippling up Price's spine as she listened. *"I'm not going to walk out of here, I'm going to fly. Kill me now, and I just come back. The Wild Hunt continues."*

She hadn't heard it the first time because Kurtzman had been routing half a dozen frequencies through his command post. But the computer had sorted the conversation between Striker and the alleged Huntsman and mastered it into a separate audio file. The muffled and flat crack of the small automatic she'd used to kill herself didn't even sound threatening in the computer lab.

Price drew her finger across her throat, and Kurtzman stopped the recording. Glancing at the far end of the room, she studied the wall screen that filled the room from floor to ceiling. A signature in the lower right-hand corner labeled the transmission feeding through the circuitry as the property of CBS News. The reporter was evidently tense as he stood in front of the Lion's Gate on Via Dolorosa. Wind whipped at the light jacket he wore and bared the wiring to the microphone he held. Dark hollows showed under his eyes in spite of the makeup. The past few days leading up to the peace talks had been filled with talk of assassins and bombs. His voice was calm and level as he spoke, but it was nothing Price hadn't already been hearing.

"What have you got on Annalee MacPherson?" she asked.

"We're still digging," Kurtzman answered. He gazed out over the three other people in the room working at separate computer consoles that fed back into his.

To his left was Carmen Delahunt, the fiery redhead they'd recruited from FBI headquarters in Quantico.

"Carmen," Kurtzman called out over the intercom system.

"Yes."

"I need an update."

The redhead turned and faced Kurtzman and Price. She slipped a headset on. "Coming at you now."

Price looked down at the trio of monitors spread across Kurtzman's desk. A picture of Annalee MacPherson popped into being through a mist of fritzing pixels. It was a publicity still, head and shoulders, with every hair in place. She'd been a good-looking woman, with long brunette hair, even teeth, a good tan and hazel eyes. Red was a power color for her, and the blouse she was wearing in the photo told Price the woman had known it. The mission controller had a hard time matching the voice she'd just heard to the woman she saw before her.

"It's starting to come apart now," Delahunt said.

"She was an impostor?" Price asked.

Delahunt shook her head. "It looks like it went even further than that. From what I can see, now that I know what kind of hard look to take at MacPherson, it appears that the woman never existed. Searching through her background reads like your typical Charles Dickens novel—parents dead, siblings dead, no known close relatives."

A list of documents slithered across the monitor screen: birth certificate, motor-vehicle registration, doctors' and medical reports, and other incidentals that made up the paper chain of a person's life.

"I've been able to verify most of the information over the past three years, though," Delahunt said. "She's put in time among the living."

Price checked the detailed bio provided in the documentation, comparing it to the mental file she had of the Huntsman's known activities. There were some glaring inconsistencies, and although the assassin had the reputation of being in more than one place at a time, the same couldn't be said for Annalee Mac-Pherson. "Her life has been verified for the past three years."

Delahunt didn't hesitate. "Yes."

"How?"

"Primarily through doctors' and dentists' care. I checked them through her insurance."

"When did the insurance kick in?"

"Three years ago."

Price glanced at the bio. According to the time line they'd established in the investigation of the reporter, MacPherson had been working at another small underground newspaper in Northern Ireland. "Was the insurance offered by her employer?"

"No. It was a policy she took out on herself."

"Her present employer didn't offer insurance?"

"No."

Price glanced at Delahunt. "What was Mac-Pherson's current yearly income?"

"Coming up."

Price studied the screen and saw the figures materialize. "And how much was the monthly premium on the insurance policy?"

The second figure rippled onto the screen under the previous information. The amount was almost a fifth of the woman's income.

"Did she use the policy much?" Price asked.

"No. From what I've been able to turn up, it was predominantly used for annual and semiannual checkups and maintenance."

"No injuries?"

Delahunt consulted her own screen. "A broken thumb. Seventeen months ago. It required setting and a cast for four weeks."

Kurtzman checked the Huntsman's file. "That's about the time frame the Huntsman was supposed to have killed three American business developers trying to get a foot in the door in Serbo-Croatia. Those assassinations were more indicative of the Huntsman's style—choosing something from the immediate area to carry out his handiwork."

Price remembered the killings from the file. One of the Americans had been strangled with her own panty hose. Another had been killed with his fountain pen through the nostril and up into the brain. The third had been killed when a light fixture, removed from the wall, had been shoved into the shower with him. Although proficient with any number of weapons, the Huntsman preferred to carry out his assignments with a variety of means he—or she, Price amended silently—exploited at the scene. "What about in October of last year?" she asked.

That was when the Huntsman was supposed to have taken a bullet in the chest in Barcelona.

Delahunt shook her head. "Nothing."

"Fine," Price said. "In case Striker is able to get away from Yellowfox Farm with the body, have a complete medical history, including dental visits, ready for comparison to the person he brought down."

"Right."

Kurtzman turned to face Price. "An insurance policy is a pretty cheap investment to make for bona fides."

"I know," the mission controller replied, glancing back at the wall screen at the far end of the room. The scene had changed, depicting a weather satellite view of the North Pacific Ocean. Black and green markings outlined the land and the sea, and bilious red whirlpools with yellow flotsam denoted the storm that had coasted up from Hawaii and had settled into the area where Able Team was waiting to go into action. "What about the other reference Striker gave us concerning the Wild Hunt?"

"I've had Hunt working on that one." Kurtzman touched another toggle on the intercom switchboard.

Seated on the right side of the room, Huntington Wethers pushed his glasses up to his brow and rubbed his eyes tiredly. An ex-professor of cybernetics at Berkeley, Wethers hadn't been trained in the espionage field and had only trod vicariously in it through books by John le Carré and others before being recruited by Kurtzman. He thrust an unlighted briarwood between his teeth and crossed his arms over his chest. "So far I've only come up with one possibility regarding the Wild Hunt, assuming a capital *W* and a capital *H*. But you've got to remember that this could be something that was coined along with the Huntsman's name."

"Leeway," Kurtzman said affectionately. "Every ivory-tower dweller I've ever known has always tried to buy himself some running room before answering questions."

"Yeah, well this one's a little out of my field," Wethers said. "Ask me anything you want about silicon chips and I'll give you the particulars." He glanced at his notes. "I referenced the Library of

Congress, the New York Public Library, the Center for Research Libraries in Chicago and the Newberry Library, also in Chicago, because I thought the term might either be literary or historical. I came up with this." He tapped his keyboard.

Price leaned over Kurtzman's shoulder and watched as a black-and-white illustration took shape on the center monitor screen.

A man sat astride a great rearing horse, a naked blade in one hand and a broad-brimmed hat obscuring his features. He wore black leather that hung loose on his sallow flesh. At the horse's hooves were a pack of snarling dogs that were half again the size of most canines. Behind the rider were at least a dozen other men, clothed in black, as well. A flock of owls rode the air of the moonless night spread out over him like an umbrella.

"Several mythologies have their version of the Wild Hunt," Wethers said in a practiced orator's voice. "Germany, Scandinavia, Scotland, Wales and England. Just to name a few. It appears the Huntsman's name derived more from these folktales than the CIA and international police agencies gave credit to."

The monitor shifted, showing another black-clad horseman guiding his animal through a tangle of wolflike shadows with gleaming fangs and red eyes.

"But never before was the term Wild Hunt used," Wethers said. "At least, not in any of the records we've been privy to. The Wild Hunt was always led by the Huntsman, though he had a dozen or so men with him. There was always one central figure. He was the incarnation of Death, a Death that came for his victims with a cold and triumphant yell."

The monitor screen changed again, showing a cowering peasant pulling his frayed cloak tightly about him as another interpretation of the Huntsman held a bundle out to him in one black-gloved fist.

"One of the stories I turned up from Devon told of a farmer who demanded the Huntsman give him one of the animals tied to the saddle pommel for his own family's cooking pot. The Huntsman is said to have laughed and tossed a parcel to the farmer, then rode off. When the farmer opened the package, he found the cold and blue body of his infant son inside. Panicked, he threw it aside and ran home as quickly as possible. Once he got there, his wife met him at the door holding their child who'd died in the night."

Remembering the list of carnage done in the Huntsman's name, Price felt that a more fitting name couldn't have been chosen. She stared at the eerie picture Wethers had turned up in his search.

"The Huntsman had many names," the ex-professor said. "In Scandinavia and Germany, the Norse and Teutonic people called him Woden, which later became translated to Odin. In Wales he was known as Gwyn ap Nudd, king of the underworld. The English alternately assumed him to be King Herla, King Arthur, or Herne, a huntsman who hanged himself in Windsor Forest and had to ride forever to pay for the suicide."

"All of which means that the guy, or guys, or women we're after is or are well-read," Kurtzman said. He tapped the keyboard and banished the disturbing image from the electronic medium, but not from Price's mind.

The mission controller considered the last words the woman had spoken before taking her own life. *"Kill me now, and I just come back. The Wild Hunt continues."* Fueled by Wethers's report and the gruesome pictures, her imagination formed images of the woman rising from the dead and creeping up on Striker while he had his back turned. She tried to force the thoughts to the back of her mind, but she had trouble. She didn't really believe in the supernatural, but a flicker of her childhood interest remained, and all the Intel on the Huntsman suggested something beyond mortal ken.

"Feed everything you've got into the main files," Price said. "Maybe it'll give us something else to work with later on."

Wethers nodded and bent to the task.

Price turned her attention to Kurtzman. "We need a coroner in England. If that backup team was at Yellowfox Farm to bring out the Huntsman's body in the event of death, I want to know why as soon as possible."

"Akira," Kurtzman called out.

"Yo." The last member of the Bear's elite group occupied the desk just in front of the wall screen. Lean and wiry, dressed in shredded jeans and a black T-shirt, Akira Tokaido was the most unconventional cybernetic spy Kurtzman had brought in to the Farm. Not trained through any formal schooling, Tokaido was a wild-card hacker who had an affinity for cybernetics systems. He wore a compact CD player on his right thigh in a gunslinger-style holster that undoubtedly cranked out the latest in heavy metal.

"Find me a doctor in England capable of performing an autopsy outside conventional hospitals who has ties to American espionage agencies."

"You got it, boss."

Kurtzman tapped keys. "Ten more minutes, Able Team should be making contact with that Russian arms shipment."

Price checked her watch. Carl Lyons had radioed that they were going to go for the interception in spite of the inclement weather. She shoved her mind into another gear, readying herself for the set of problems that that exercise would bring about.

"All this talk about the Wild Hunt," Kurtzman said quietly, "makes it sound like we're putting out an APB on Death."

"Yeah," Price said, and found her voice more dry than she'd expected. "But this is only one of the present incarnations. Nothing we can't handle." She wished she felt as confident as she sounded, but Striker was running for his life, and Able Team and Phoenix Force were just about to step into the breach at her direction.

**4**

Carl Lyons stared hard into the storm-tossed sea and held on to the Canadian Coast Guard cutter's railing. A few of the waves broke over the bow and splashed back over him. It didn't matter, though, because he was already drenched. He wore a thick woolen pea coat against the chill of the wind, and a San Francisco 49ers ball cap pulled down tight.

"This," Rosario Blancanales said at his side, "is going to be a royal bitch." The rain had plastered his hair to his head, and the long coat he wore whirled around him. Built stocky and possessing a low center of gravity, he seemed to have no problems with the pitching and rolling of the cutter. But beneath those aristocratic features that could take on the hint of a street savage when the role called for it, Lyons thought he could detect the slightest tinge of green. He was called the Politician because of his cool head and ability to be—more or less—whatever his audience believed him to be.

Lyons glanced toward the pilothouse and saw Dimitri Golodkin make his way down the companionway. Even in the uneven illumination of the running lights, the big ex-LAPD cop could see that things weren't progressing exactly as the Russian policeman might have wanted.

"Now there," Blancanales said, "comes a truly sad face." He had to yell to be heard above the gale force of the whipping winds, but his voice didn't carry to the Russian.

Golodkin made the railing with difficulty. He was a scarecrow of a man, and his coat looked much too large for him. His fur cap was pulled down low and threatened to blend in with his eyebrows. "The help I expected from the Russian mainland isn't going to be coming," he stated simply in good English. "They've had trouble with the weather."

"No backup," Lyons said with a tight, white grin. "I've played a few refrains on that one myself."

"You're still intending to confront these people?"

A bolt of lightning streaked across the skies, followed almost immediately by a crashing crescendo of thunder.

"I didn't come all this way to go fishing," the big Able Team warrior replied. "And the way my ass has been frozen these past couple of hours, it's going to take some action to thaw it out."

"What about the Canadians? I haven't told them yet."

"Selling people," Blancanales stated. "That's my specialty." He clapped the Russian cop on the back and made his way toward the lower cabin where the Canadian Coast Guard captain was briefing his team.

"The Canadians aren't going to want that arms shipment hitting their shores," Lyons said, "and they couldn't get out the helicopters we'd asked for."

Golodkin took a crumpled cigarette pack from his pocket and tried to light one. Failing, he tossed the whole pack overboard and sighed.

"Chewing tobacco," Lyons suggested. "No matter what Mother Nature does, you can still enjoy it."

"I shouldn't even be smoking. I'd quit until this case."

Lyons nodded. He knew from the Intel Price and Kurtzman had gathered for the strike that Golodkin had put in four very hard months to make his case against the Russian illegal-arms dealers. The man had also lost his partner in a bloody street battle in Kamchatskiy three weeks earlier, while trying to apprehend the shipment before it left the Commonwealth. Hard work in the trenches during the following days had turned up the lead to the *Agnes Green,* a freighter shipping from Taiwan.

"Let's take a look at the radar screen and see where we stand," Lyons suggested. He led the way to the pilothouse across the slippery deck.

It felt good to be out of the pounding rain, and the warmth of the pilothouse heaters was welcome relief. Lyons leaned over the radar screen.

Hermann Schwarz stood beside the radar operator. He wore a yellow rain slicker that was unbuckled and revealed the olive-drab Property of the U.S. Army sweatshirt he had on underneath. Lean and athletic, the third member of Able Team had been part of Mack Bolan's Pen-Team Able, as had Blancanales, in the hellish days of Vietnam. Schooled in deadly warfare and covert operations, he'd earned the nickname Gadgets from his ability to put together deadly devices from everyday items.

"The *Agnes Green?*" Lyons asked.

Schwarz nodded and tapped a green glowing blip on the radar screen, earning a reproachful look from the young coast guardsman assigned to the station.

"How far away?"

Schwarz held his thumb and forefinger apart and up. "Looks like about two inches to me."

"Terrific. Give me something I can work with."

"Approximately seven knots," the young seaman answered.

"ETA?"

"Fifteen, twenty minutes. In this weather it's hard to say. Captain Rycliff has already been notified. He's on his way up."

Lyons studied the sweep of the radar arm as it skated around the greenish circle. He knew the Canadian Coast Guard cutter's sensors had been tied into the weather satellite that had been tapped by Kurtzman from Stony Man Farm. "Can they track us?"

"Yeah," Schwarz replied. "Right now they think we're a pleasure yacht from Vancouver that got trapped out in the storm."

"Do they believe it?"

"They seem to."

Captain James Rycliff walked through the door, a tight expression on his weathered face.

"Your team isn't coming?" Rycliff asked Golodkin.

The Russian faced him squarely. "No."

"If your estimates concerning the crew of the *Agnes Green* are correct, we're going to be outgunned almost three to one if we go ahead with this encounter."

"The estimates are correct," Golodkin said. "But we're not going to be as severely outnumbered as the citizens of your own country if those arms are allowed to land there. You tell me how dangerous these gangs of yours will be when armed with AK-47s and RPG-7 rocket launchers."

"Your military should have kept tighter safeguards on their munitions," Rycliff accused.

Golodkin showed no evidence of being insulted. "My country and several of her neighbors are in a state of turmoil these days. I can't help that, and neither can many defenseless citizens. But I came here and told you of our problems with the stolen munitions after conferring with the Americans, in the hopes of preventing bloodshed from washing over into your streets. How do you propose to handle the situation?"

"Waiting until they get into port is no answer," Blancanales said reasonably. "The storm is going to hold for hours after their arrival. Even if they don't off-load somewhere along the way, there's no way they're going to give up without a fight. Here, on the open sea, we might be better equipped to contain the violence without causing an international incident with other properties being destroyed."

Lyons knew the coast-guard captain had no real choice. The *Agnes Green*'s destination was Vancouver, and the city thrived on tourist and international trade. An incident of this sort could cause a black eye that could take a long time to get over.

Rycliff thought it over quickly as he glanced at the glowing blip on the radar screen. His men inside the pilothouse watched him. Lyons knew the man's decision before he spoke.

"Do you Americans still want a part of this?" the captain asked.

"Didn't come all this way to warm a bench, captain," Lyons answered. "But I might suggest something in the way of a more creative strategy when we approach them."

"I'm open to suggestion, Mr. Lancaster," Rycliff said, using Lyons's cover name, "but we still have rules in our police work here. We don't open fire without hailing our suspects first."

"Right." Lyons waved to his teammates and the Russian cop and led the way outside. He clipped the ear-throat headset into place and shifted from the shipboard frequency to the tach channel Able Team had agreed to use for private communications. "Gadgets, have you got your little nasties rigged?"

Schwarz held up a remote-control device. "Yeah."

Lyons ascended the metal steps to the flybridge. He could feel the cutter coming about beneath him. "Did the captain or his men notice?"

"Did he mention them to you?"

"No."

"Then I guess not."

Lyons took a pair of infrared binoculars from inside his coat pocket and scanned the open sea. The *Agnes Green* was nowhere to be seen.

"At best, Ironman," Schwarz said more seriously, "it's only going to buy a little time."

"Then it's up to us to make every second count," Lyons replied. He swept the field glasses across the dark water again and spotted the freighter this time, looking like a metal skeleton coasting across the sea when lightning flared across the sky.

He reached down and keyed open the metal equipment case they'd brought on board and secured to the flybridge less than an hour earlier. He shrugged out of the pea coat and lashed it to the railing, leaving the black windbreaker with POLICE stamped across the back in inches-high phosphorous letters. He carried the .45 Colt Government Model in shoulder leather and the .357 Magnum Colt Python on his hip. He took a Barrett Model 82 Light Fifty sniper rifle from the equipment case and checked the 10x scope. Shrugging one arm out of the windbreaker for a moment, he pulled on a sling that supported a Mossberg Model 500 Bullpup 12 combat shotgun with a mounted flashlight for night firing.

In addition to their Beretta 92-S side arms, Blancanales and Schwarz also carried H&K MP-5 SD-3 submachine guns. Extra clips filled their pockets.

As the coast-guard cutter neared the suspect freighter, two deckhands clambered up the metal steps and ripped the tarp back from a swivel-mounted 20 mm cannon. Fifty-caliber machine guns were mounted fore and aft on the cutter, and other crews were already tending to those.

The *Agnes Green*'s running lights were visible to the naked eye now, and the jagged streaks of lightning illuminated the activity across her decks.

"I don't think they're buying it anymore that we're a pleasure boat," Lyons said dryly.

He accessed the ship-to-ship frequency Rycliff was using to send his message to the freighter's skipper.

The channel hissed and sputtered, but the coast-guard captain's words were intelligible.

"*Agnes Green,* this is the Canadian Coast Guard. Over."

There was no response.

Rycliff repeated his message. While he talked, the freighter made a slight course correction and tried to pull away from the closing cutter. Coast-guard searchlights played over the water and the freighter with hit-or-miss regularity, creating shifting pools of white.

Lyons settled in behind his weapon and brought the scope to his eye. It was difficult timing the pitch and yaw of the cutter to the rise and fall of the freighter. The distance, he guessed because the night and conditions made the estimate hard, was around seven hundred yards, well within the Barrett's capabilities. He targeted the wheelhouse as best as he could and waited.

"*Agnes Green,*" Rycliff transmitted again, "this is Captain James Rycliff of the Canadian Coast Guard. You will heave to and prepare to be boarded in compliance with international maritime law-enforcement regulations."

"About now, in favor of clearer communications and to establish a proper frame of reference for negotiations," Blancanales said, "I'd be putting a cannon shot across their bow."

"Tell me about it," Lyons commented quietly. His finger took up trigger slack on the big sniper rifle. "Gadgets?"

"Ready."

A flurry of activity was unleashed across the deck of the freighter. Canvases were pulled back from three different sections.

Lyons strained hard through the scope to make out the details. A heartbeat later all uncertainty was removed when the thunderous roar of an artillery piece was heard. A puff of gray smoke twisted out behind the big muzzle.

"Sweet Lord!" Blancanales exclaimed. "That's a big gun."

"No shit, Sherlock," Schwarz growled.

The warbling howl of the incoming shell split the air. It landed and detonated only a few yards from the cutter. A spiraling twist of white spume slathered up over the vessel's decks.

Switching objectives, Lyons kept both eyes open as he sighted in on the gun crew, walking the barrel down during a swell of the ocean waves, then focusing on the scope. He fired two shots. The big Barrett thudded painfully against his shoulder because it was hard to brace himself and adjust at the same time. At least one of the rounds was on the money because a gunner was ripped from his post.

Lyons keyed the headset. "They've got us outgunned, too, Rycliff. Even if we tried to cut and run from this engagement, they've probably got the range to sink us before we could go far."

"I know," the captain said tersely. "We're going to attempt to get in under her guns. Stand ready."

The cutter surged with renewed power, almost coming up out of the water as her tail twisted and she drove for the freighter.

It was a gutsy play and Lyons knew it. He stayed behind the .50-caliber sniper rifle and provided as much covering fire as he could.

Another round from one of the freighter's cannon slammed into the upper aft bow of the cutter. The resulting explosion did little more than cosmetic damage to the vessel, but the shrapnel that ripped free cleared the 20 mm cannon mounted on the flybridge. One man went over the side without a word, and the other smashed up against the tower.

Blancanales ran to the wounded sailor's side and attempted to staunch his wounds. Schwarz raced to man the cannon, joined by Golodkin.

Ramming a fresh clip into the Barrett, Lyons saw the distance separating the cutter from the freighter had dwindled to less than four hundred yards. He shifted his aim back to the wheelhouse and pulled the trigger repeatedly when he was sure he had it in his sights. Jagged streaks of lightning revealed the massive holes the .50-caliber rounds ripped through the Plexiglas windows.

Someone had thought to douse the freighter's running lights, and the vessel knifed through the rolling sea dark and silent, as the winds ripped away the sounds of the straining diesels.

Schwarz and Golodkin worked in tandem to hurl 20 mm rounds at the *Agnes Green*. Flaming bits of wreckage tumbled into the sky and across the sea in two places as their marksmanship improved. The fore .50-caliber machine gun was chattering with deadly enthusiasm, and sparks jumped from the freighter's metallic skin in dozens of places. The cutter's aft gun crew worked sporadically as their vessel came about broadside.

Captain Rycliff's bellowed orders carried over the headset frequency. Despite the tension of the moment, the coast-guard captain ran on adrenaline and cool nerve.

Muzzle-flashes lined the freighter's railings as the deckhands took part in the running gun battle. Lyons couldn't begin to estimate the numbers. The coast-guard cutter was beginning to feel the effects of the small-arms fire even though the *Agnes Green* was no longer able to bring her cannon to bear.

The big Able Team warrior ran through the clip in the Barrett, scoring six hits out of the eleven rounds, then dropped the weapon in the equipment case. Rycliff had assembled a boarding party in the cutter's prow, and Lyons intended to be part of it. He hooked his feet on the outside railings of the ladder, then used his hands and slid to the deck. Schwarz, Blancanales and Golodkin were on his heels.

The cutter was within thirty yards of the freighter and closing. The bigger ship looked almost elegant cutting through the water as whitecaps spilled back from her prow. But she couldn't maneuver quickly because of her tonnage. It had occurred to Lyons that the freighter captain might attempt to ram them, but it would have been like a dinosaur trying to swat a road runner.

The freighter's crew was fighting for its life, and had massed against the railing. Small-arms fire rained on the cutter in spite of the return fire from the coast-guard's hands.

Lyons fired the Mossberg Bullpup as fast as he could, laying down a screen of double-aught buckshot that ripped into flesh and drove the gunners back. Rycliff's crew readied the ropes they'd prepared for forcible boarding. Two lines were tied to a hemp fishing net, leading to a pair of grappling hooks loaded into two harpoon guns that had been mounted before leaving harbor.

The cutter powered to within twenty yards and came about broadside to the freighter. The fore and aft cannon were pounding into the *Agnes Green*'s superstructure, wrecking her exposed electronics.

Lyons reloaded under cover of the cutter's railing.

Rycliff was a commanding presence on the deck. His voice boomed out above the confusion. "Ready harpoon guns."

"Aye, sir. Harpoon guns ready."

"Fire!"

"Harpoons away!"

The harpoon guns belched like giant trucks letting off air pressure. Electronically controlled to fire simultaneously, both coils of rope began paying out at once, followed by the skein of fishing net.

Lyons tapped the headset button. "Gadgets."

"Go."

"It's time." Lyons watched as the grappling hooks sailed over the freighter's railing. The ropes fell back toward the sea for a moment, then caught, suspending the fishing net down the side of the bigger ship. The deck, rearing and pitching across the waves, was still thirty feet above the cutter.

"Fire in the hole!" Schwarz warned.

A colorful hell opened up above the freighter and the cutter. Flares and rocket-powered incendiaries took flight and turned the black sky red, green and amber. Schwarz had wired various launchers around the cutter with the intent of providing a moment or so of distraction at a critical time. It was something Rycliff with all his spit-and-polish command wouldn't have condoned. But Lyons had figured it would come in handy. If not, it would have made a hell of a celebratory salute if an easy victory had been in the offing.

Still at speed, though, the freighter was starting to leave the pinwheeling flares and rockets behind, but the distraction had earned precious time.

Letting the Mossberg hang from the sling, Lyons took a running start and launched himself at the hanging fishing net barely ten yards away. His shoulders flamed painfully from suddenly taking his weight as he knotted his fingers in the net and started to climb. The net slipped for a moment as more of the coast-guard crew joined him, then held.

He scrambled up the netting as quickly as possible, drawing the Colt Government Model as he reached for the railing. One of the freighter crew looked down at him and brought an AK-47 to his shoulder.

Lyons swung to the side and fired the .45 point-blank, catching his target in the face. The man jerked back out of sight. On the deck, Lyons slid across the wet surface and came up against one of the fire fighting stations. He took a grenade from a Windbreaker pocket, pulled the pin and flipped the bomb toward the group of men massed near the pressure and vacuum relief valves.

The grenade bounced once then exploded in the air, clearing the area.

Lyons provided covering fire as two of Rycliff's sailors pulled the ropes tied into the fishing net flush to the climbing surface butted up against the deck. He saw Gadgets and the Politician come over in the next wave, followed closely by the Russian cop.

"Ironman," Blancanales called over the headset as he flattened himself against the foremast.

"Here."

"Intact?"

"All the good stuff, anyway." Lyons watched as the freighter's crew tried in vain to wage a holding action against the coast-guard sailors. Gunfire echoed along the vessel's steel deck. "You guys have below deck in case they try to scuttle the holds. Dimitri and I will take the wheelhouse."

"Roger," Schwarz answered. He and the Politician went into motion.

"Ready?" Lyons asked the Russian cop.

Golodkin tightened his grip on the assault rifle and nodded.

"Let's do it." Lyons erupted from his position and fired two quick rounds into the three men who suddenly confronted him. The double-aught buckshot blew them down, and the Able Team warrior vaulted across their falling corpses.

Lyons led the way, racing past the tank hatches and heading for the wheelhouse at the other end of the freighter.

A phalanx of gunners hovering around the lifeboat station sent Lyons and Golodkin ducking for cover. The Russian provided defensive fire while Lyons drew the Colt Python. Taking deliberate aim, hampered by the continued pitch of the freighter, the big ex-cop sighted on the lifeboat's gas tanks. Besides being equipped with a sail and oars, it was also outfitted with a small gasoline engine.

He fired twice. Both rounds punctured the gas tanks without igniting. Fuel leaked and splattered onto the deck and across two of the men hiding there. Reaching into his windbreaker, he pulled out a hand flare, broke the seal to start the ignition, then flung the fiery stick toward the lifeboat.

The flare rolled and skated across the deck and slid into the pool of gasoline. Flames whooshed into life, burning cherry-red and yellow as they reached for the lifeboat. The two sailors also caught fire.

Lyons took a two-handed grip on his pistol and put mercy rounds through one of the men. Before he could get the other, the man fell over the side, a human comet that was extinguished by the black sea.

A burst from Golodkin's assault rifle chewed into the remainder of the group and took down two more. The three survivors threw down their weapons and prostrated themselves on the deck.

"Hey!" Lyons called to two coast-guard sailors who were nearing his position. "These men are ready to be taken into custody." When they'd moved up to cover the prisoners, he and Golodkin moved on.

Lyons took the steps leading up the wheelhouse two and three at a time, a pistol in each hand. He slid twice, coming to a painful stop against the railing. When he reached the door, he glanced at the Russian. "I'm going high."

"I will take low."

"Let's do it." Lyons lifted a big boot and slammed it into the door. It shivered as the lock shelled out, then banged backward.

Four sailors manned the stations, including the captain, a grizzly of a man with a dark beard and a stained Harvard yachting cap. He held a Skorpion machine pistol in one massive hand and fired it toward the door, brass spilling from the ejector port as bullets bit into the woodwork.

Bringing both pistols to bear, Lyons shot the captain six times in the chest as he went through the door. He was aware of Golodkin firing methodical bursts. The navigator and pilot dropped away as their weapons fell silent. The captain stumbled backward, his machine pistol scoring the ceiling.

A bullet plucked at Lyons's windbreaker as he turned on the last man. He stared down the sailor's muzzle as he fired, felt the heat of a bullet fan by his cheek, then watched as his rounds took the man below the collarbone and knocked him back against the helm.

Moving quickly, Lyons dragged the corpse out of the way and cut the freighter's engines. The gunfire aboard the vessel was more sporadic now, and the absence of the dull roar and shiver of the diesels was noticeable.

Lyons keyed the headset. "Pol. Gadgets."

"Go," Blancanales responded.

"The hold?" Lyons crossed the wheelhouse to the door and went down the companionway.

"We own it, Ironman."

Schwarz broke in. "We might have a problem."

"What?" Lyons asked. Golodkin was right behind him.

The deck was littered with bodies and flames. The coast-guard cutter was off the port side, slowing its pace to draw up against the stalling freighter.

"The shipment doesn't appear to be all here," Schwarz answered.

A shadow jerked to Lyons's right. The Able Team warrior flicked on the combat shotgun's flashlight and dropped the beam's ellipse over the sailor who was trying to raise his weapon. Without hesitation, the sailor dropped his rifle and raised his hands. Lyons waved him to the deck, and Golodkin swiftly handcuffed him.

"Where are you?" Lyons asked.

"Amidships."

Taking the nearest hatch, Lyons lifted it and went through, using the shotgun's flashlight to show him the way. The hold stank of rusting metal, brine and countless odors he couldn't identify. He could tell at a glance that the wooden crates marked FARM EQUIPMENT weren't near the number the Russian police had briefed them to expect.

Schwarz and Blancanales stood in the middle of the crates with crowbars and heavy-duty flashlights. An electric torch aimed at the steel beams overhead resembled a miniature sun in the darkness. Nails screeched as Gadgets levered up the cover of another crate.

Lyons shoved it aside once it was free. Golodkin leaned forward, his face tight, and ran a long arm through the foam-pellet packing. A dozen AK-47 assault rifles were packed inside with a box of Russian antipersonnel grenades. The oily sheen on the metal gleamed.

"Some of the crates actually do contain farm equipment," Blancanales reported.

Lyons glanced around the crates. "We're way off the mark from what we were told to expect."

"No kidding," Schwarz said in disgust. "If those reports were on the money, there's still a lot of hardware out there making its way into the hands of the Loc-Tu gangs who are causing problems in Vancouver, Toronto and Montreal."

Lyons kicked the crate in exasperation. The Loc-Tu Triad had a stranglehold on the organized Oriental crime scene in major Canadian cities. No longer content to stay in Chinatown, the Triad was using terrorist tactics to snag a larger piece of the pie.

At the far end of the hold, Rycliff led a small contingent of coast guardsmen into the hold. The captain gazed at the crates. "Did we get it?"

"Some of it," Lyons said. "According to our Intel, there's no way this is all of it."

Rycliff's face hardened. "I lost two damned fine men on this operation, and you're telling me it wasn't a success?"

"It was half a success," Lyons argued.

"One Loc-Tu gang member on the streets with a gun is a failure in my book," Rycliff said.

"Mine, too," Golodkin added quietly. His eyes burned with harsh inner fires.

"Maybe there's an answer to our problems," Blancanales said. He grabbed a handcuffed man from the floor and shoved him forward. "Meet Christos, the ship's first officer."

The first officer wore dark clothing and a black watch cap. Thick brows made his forehead seem more prominent, and his coarse mustache looked as if it grew out of his hawk nose. At least part of his parentage had roots in the Middle East.

Lyons invaded the man's personal space and locked eyes with him. Christos flinched, then caught himself and stiffened his back.

"Where are the rest of the guns?" Lyons demanded.

"To hell with you," the man said in accented English. "Arrest me. All they can do is deport me back to Turkey as an undesirable alien."

"Maybe that's all the Canadian government can do," Lyons growled, "but I'm not the Canadian government." He grabbed the man by the jacket lapels and hauled him up the companionway, using his greater weight to drag the man when he pulled back.

Lyons put Christos in a lockstep hold and marched the man across the deck in view of the coast-guard personnel and the captured freighter hands now standing at attention. Rain swept across the vessel's deck, and she rode out loose across the rolling waves.

Handling his prisoner roughly, Lyons slammed him up against the anchor windlass and mooring winch with enough force to drive the air from the man's lungs. Before Christos could act, Lyons had him handcuffed to the anchor line.

"What the hell do you think you're doing?" Rycliff demanded.

Lyons turned to face the coast-guard captain and set the anchor controls into motion. "I'm getting some answers."

The line paid out and dragged a screaming Christos toward the railing. Uncertain looks flickered across the faces of the coast-guard sailors. A protest started among the ranks of the captured vessel's deckhands.

"You can't do that," Rycliff said.

The winch motor shrilled in Lyons's ears. Schwarz and Blancanales stepped forward with their submachine guns canted across their chests, making it obvious they were backing their teammate's play.

Christos tried to hold back from the railing, but the weight of the man-size anchor dragged him over without any problem. He screamed, hoarse and frightened.

"Sure I can," Lyons replied. He yanked the control lever and stopped the chain from feeding through. "Would you rather that half a shipment of guns hit Vancouver and made their way east?"

Rycliff's face tightened.

Leaving the coast-guard captain, Lyons walked to the edge of the railing and waved Schwarz to the anchor controls. He slipped the flashlight from the Mossberg Bullpup and flicked it on. Callously he played the beam over the dark water waiting yards below and the whitecaps breaking against the prow of the freighter. Then he shined it in the first officer's eyes.

"Your choice," Lyons said in a cold voice.

Christos hung painfully by his wrists, suspended from the anchor and thumping solidly against the freighter's hull.

"I put you down," Lyons yelled to be heard over the crash of the waves, "and you stay down. I'll move on to the ship's purser and the cook if I have to. What's it going to be?''

"There was another ship," Christos bellowed back. "Get me up."

"What was the ship?"

"The *India Moon*. She took a longer route around because we thought the Russians were aware of us, but we laid back so our arrival would be about the same. With the storm, though, we got behind. She should already be putting into port."

Lyons looked back at the coast-guard captain. Rycliff was already issuing orders over the handheld walkie-talkie he carried. The big Able Team warrior looked at Schwarz and nodded. The anchor chain clanked as it pulled back up.

Hauling Christos to his feet, Lyons said, "Now I want the name of the guy you were supposed to meet up with in Vancouver."

## 5

Mack Bolan worked the lock of the back door of the copy store with ease. When the final tumbler of the lock fell into place, he dropped his pick into his pocket, twisted the knob and walked inside. The telephone-directory advertisement had listed fax capabilities among the shop's services.

He used a penflash to maneuver in the cramped space, finally reaching the machine he needed.

In the past hour, Dover had come alive. Roving police squads scoured the city for the assassins who'd tried to kill the prime minister. Hovercraft arrivals had been temporarily suspended, and all roads leading from the city had been blocked off.

The escape from Yellowfox Farm had been a near thing. He'd liberated a sedan from a cabin a mile or so from the farm. He'd managed two more swaps before ending up with the Citroën parked outside that held the dead woman in the trunk.

Once the fax machine was operational, he picked up the connected phone and punched in a local number that was being used by Stony Man Farm in the event of an emergency. He listened to it ring, then noticed the slight clicks that signified that the call was being forwarded to different cutouts leading eventually back to the Farm.

Barbara Price answered the call on the fourth ring.

"Me," Bolan said, glancing down at the fax machine. "I've got something for you."

"Where are you?" the mission controller asked.

Bolan gave her the name and number of the copy shop.

"Send it. I'll call you back."

The warrior said "Right" and broke the connection. Reaching inside his bomber jacket, he took out two sheets of paper he'd prepared earlier. Using a can of shoe polish he'd purchased at an all-night convenience store, he'd taken the dead woman's prints.

Both papers fed quickly through the fax machine, and two minutes later the phone rang.

The warrior scooped up the receiver and shut off the fax machine.

"We got them," Price said. "Do they belong to the woman?"

"Yeah. It's still possible somebody slipped in a ringer."

"I'll have the comparisons done in a couple minutes."

Bolan moved toward the front of the shop and watched through the window, standing so he couldn't be easily seen. Traffic was negligible, which was one of the reasons he'd chosen this location.

"Chances are, it's MacPherson," Price stated. In terse sentences, she revealed the information about the woman that Kurtzman's team had uncovered. "It's also possible that she's not the Huntsman."

"She was tonight," Bolan said with conviction. "What about the reference to the Wild Hunt?"

"Mythology. Irish, Germanic, Scottish, take your pick. It refers to the harvesting of souls by a group of ghouls back from the dead and from hell itself."

"Has a certain lyrical ring."

"Indicates that the mind behind this is both demented and creative."

"Any progress along those lines?"

"No. We're still checking into MacPherson's background, but unless we get a break, it's going to be about as useful as Hansel and Gretel's trail of bread crumbs. I'll keep you posted."

"Do that." Bolan's attention was drawn by a sedan that coasted to a stop on the other side of the street from the car he'd taken. The lights were extinguished, and a moment later a man got out on the passenger side.

"Jack's ready to make the rendezvous when you are," Price said.

"At sea?"

"Yes."

The man who debarked from the sedan was tall and broad. A trench coat flared out around him, caught by the wind. For a moment, a hard length was revealed under the coat at the man's side.

Bolan's combat senses tingled in warning. The man didn't make a direct line for the car the warrior was using, but the Executioner sensed that the vehicle was the guy's ultimate target.

"Did you line up a medical examiner?" Bolan asked as he reached a hand under his bomber jacket and closed it around the butt of the silenced Browning Hi-Power tucked in the waistband of his pants.

"Yes. Dr. Elizabeth Parrish is standing by."

"Can she meet me at the docks in ten or fifteen minutes?"

"You're figuring on a rush job?"

"Of the quickest sort." Bolan didn't think the man was a police officer. The guy never checked the license plates. When he pulled a device out of his pocket and examined it, the warrior knew he was right. And he knew the team that had been hired to exfiltrate the Huntsman or her body hadn't given up. The guy waved to his partner. The car's lights flashed for an instant.

"Where do you want to meet her?"

Bolan named a marina on the east side of the main shipping docks. "Can she be ready to operate?"

"A full autopsy?"

"No. Just a superficial exploratory one. That corpse has a homing device in it. I'm not going to be able to break free of this net without it."

"Affirmative. I'll let her know."

"And see if Jack can dig up some sort of portable X-ray machine. We're going to have to stay mobile until we deactivate the thing."

"I'll see what I can do. There's a NATO base we might be able to work something out with, but it could delay Jack."

"I'll take the delay as long as we can preserve our anonymity." Bolan cradled the phone and walked to the front door. He took out his lock pick and swiftly worked the dead bolt. The other two locks unlatched from the inside with quiet snicks.

Out in the street, the sedan had come around in a loose 180-degree turn and parked in front of Bolan's borrowed wheels. The man at the trunk had taken a screwdriver and a hammer from his coat.

Neither man appeared to have noticed Bolan yet. The warrior kept the Browning out of sight against his leg. By coming out of the copy shop through the front door, he gave the impression of an owner running a late-night errand. He was aware that the two men had others watching them, otherwise the driver wouldn't have bothered with signaling.

Bolan walked toward them, as if he were going to cross at the corner. His eyes scanned the streets, wondering where the secondary attack was going to come from. His ears picked up the sounds of radio static bursting into life, and he knew the numbers had run thin on the play.

The sedan driver looked up at him, reaching for something lying in the passenger seat.

Without wasted motion, Bolan brought up the Browning. It bucked in his fist, and a 9 mm round drilled through the driver's forehead. He jerked to one side, his head smashing against the partially open side window, then flopped back to the steering wheel. The horn blared a heartbeat later, almost covering the echoing gunshot, and stayed on. The car bobbed into motion and narrowly missed the parked sedan as it crawled over the curb.

The second man dropped his burglary tools and tried for the Uzi on a sling under his arm.

Still on the move, the Executioner brought the Hi-Power into target acquisition and rattled off three quick shots that tracked up from the man's chest to meet his chin. The corpse was still falling backward when Bolan reached the car door.

Tires screeched at the end of the street as the warrior pulled himself behind the wheel. He glanced in the rearview mirror as he keyed the ignition.

A panel truck shot out from a nearby alley. Its headlights flashed as it heeled around and came at him, intending to cut Bolan off.

Wrenching the wheel and flooring the accelerator, the Executioner rammed his sedan into the panel truck. For a moment the bumpers locked, and the vehicles careened down the street.

Across the seat, Bolan saw the window behind the driver open suddenly and the snout of a machine pistol poke through. He tapped the brake, yanked the steering wheel to disengage the bumpers and hit the accelerator again in an evasive action.

Cutting the wheels hard to the right, he cut inside a lamppost at the corner, then felt it jar along the length of the car. Bullets exploded through the rear passenger window and splattered glass fragments all over him. He felt the warmth of blood trickle down his neck.

He took a right at the corner, heading away from the docks for the moment, pursued by the panel truck. The driver's-side headlight had been shattered, making it look like a mechanical Cyclops.

The street was narrow, lighted its entire length by only a handful of streetlights. Most of the businesses, according to the advertising Bolan was able to glimpse, had to do with the automotive industry. He eased his foot from the accelerator and let the panel truck close. Another burst of the assault rifle cleared the back glass.

Watching the oncoming loading ramp on the other side of the street, Bolan cut the steering wheel as the panel truck roared up on his left and became framed in the passenger window. The sedan lacked the true bulk it needed to muscle the panel truck over, but the warrior fired the rest of the Browning's clip into the driver's door.

Spooked and possibly injured, the panel truck's driver pulled away from the sedan. He had to have realized where he was headed a heartbeat later because the truck slammed frantically back into the sedan. The warrior held the line, and tortured metal screamed. Less than twenty yards farther on, the panel truck's left wheels hit the loading ramp.

Bolan floored the accelerator and shot away from the truck as it overturned. He watched in his rearview mirror as it sailed into the air for a moment, then landed on its side and skidded out of control, leaving a flurry of sparks in its wake.

The warrior turned another corner at the end of the street and left his pursuers behind.

BOLAN ROLLED the sedan to a stop in a vacant parking space beside the marina he'd told Price about, and switched off the engine.

A woman's shadow stood in the darkness before him. A lighter flared to life briefly as she lighted a cigarette. The features that were revealed were honest and open, and nervous. She wore a long coat over a blue blouse and a full black skirt.

"Dr. Parrish," Bolan said as he climbed out of the car.

"You're Mr. Belasko?"

"Right. We don't have much time."

"You look like you just rolled out of World War III."

"If we stand here talking, there's a chance it's going to catch up to us."

"How much trouble is this going to be?"

"The lady that sent you here made sure you had some sense of that. Just move when I do and when I tell you to, and you're going to be all right." Bolan popped the trunk latch and picked up the body. He'd wrapped it in a blanket he'd found in the trunk space. Draping the corpse over his shoulder, he grabbed the ordnance bag from the tire well and set off at a brisk pace.

Parrish hesitated only a moment. Dropping the cigarette, she crushed it underfoot and hurried after him.

Bolan searched the line of sailing vessels moored at the marina. A guard post was at the end of the pier, but the guard didn't seem interested in coming out to meet them. The warrior tossed him a cordial wave that was returned slowly.

"You know him?" Parrish asked.

"No, but he'll think I do for a while." Finding a motor sailer that looked quick enough and easy enough to operate with a two-man crew, Bolan stepped aboard. The cabin was locked. He dropped the ordnance bag and picked the lock. "Grab that bag, please."

She did.

Bolan went down into the cabin and laid the corpse on the floor and unwrapped her.

"Oh, shit," Parrish said when she saw the bullet wounds and damage inflicted by the car bumper.

Switching on his penlight, Bolan played it over the body. "You've been briefed on what we need?"

The woman nodded, her attention focused on the corpse. In the reflected light, her auburn hair held fiery highlights, falling in tight curls to trickle into her blouse collar. Her gray eyes were slightly bloodshot but moved alertly.

"For right now," the warrior said, "I need a quick examination. Somewhere on her body, there has to be some kind of radio-broadcasting unit."

"A homing device?"

"Yeah. I've been bird-dogged by a team that's supposed to get her body back or destroy it. If we don't find it, we're going to be dodging them every step of the way."

Parrish knelt by the body and began peeling the bloody garments away. "I'm going to need more light than this."

Bolan pressed the penlight into her hand. "Later. First I need to make a phone call, then get us out of the harbor before the cops or the bad guys catch up to us. I'll be back in a couple minutes."

Parrish nodded, then opened the black bag at her side and set to work.

The warrior walked back off the motor sailer and down the dock to the public phone. He placed his call, got Price and told her the radio frequency he'd be using while on the boat. After setting the pickup time for Grimaldi, he broke the connection, returned to the motor sailer, cast off and started the engines, which turned over smoothly. Within minutes he was heading out of the marina for the open sea of the English Channel.

**6**

Hayden Thone worked the rifle's bolt action with loving care. The metallic taste of the gun oil coating it filled his nostrils. He slipped his finger through the trigger guard without haste, then sighted in on the target at the far end of the shooting gallery.

Just a fraction of an inch under six feet tall, he was built like a good quarterback, with long arms, a broad frame and just enough weight to make him a good running threat on a quarterback sneak. In his late forties, age had lent a touch of gray to his temples and mustache, leaving the rest of the hair sandy colored. Crow's-feet and laugh lines that left parentheses around his narrow-lipped mouth gave him a dignified air. He wore a tan Banana Republic jacket over a white chambray shirt. A black bandanna was tied around his neck in cowboy fashion. His faded blue jeans held a crease and flared out over the cowboy boots with silver toes that encased his feet. He knew he looked good for the camera.

The audience was silent, watching with anticipation.

The scope brought the target into sharp relief. Thone knew there was no way he could miss at the distance. The gallery was ranged for pistol shooting, not rifles. But he loved the attention of the audience, so he milked it.

The gallery's other lanes were empty, with threatening silhouettes already waiting in place. Off to Thone's right, so they could view man and weapon to their best, were three cameras and the director who had been hired to shoot the footage.

Then, with the skill that had won him a gold medal in the 1972 Olympics in Munich while on the Austrian shooting and skiing teams, Thone pulled the trigger. The flat crack of the shot rang across the shooting gallery as he smoothly worked the bolt action and chambered another round. Thone operated like a machine, liquid and efficient, as he fired the four remaining bullets. He rolled easily with each recoil, always coming back to the target.

Finished, he gripped the rifle by the barrel and handed it to one of the attendants standing nearby. Applause erupted around the shooting gallery. Thone looked at Creel Springer, who was sitting in the director's chair with a look of awe on his face.

Springer was in his early twenties and still carried a teenager's slim build. His carrot-red hair was cut boot-camp short, and he sported a neatly trimmed beard. Hazel eyes moved restlessly behind round-lensed glasses and under the bill of a plain, black ball cap.

"Wow!" the young director exclaimed as he pushed himself out of the folding chair. He waved to the cameras without looking at them. "Cut. Damn, that was frigging fantastic." He mimed holding a rifle and shooting at the target at the far end of the room. "Like you were Lee Marvin or Chuck Bronson in one of those old Westerns. Get the hell out of Dodge! Geez, that held energy.''

Thone forced a smile. He didn't like the director, and hated being around a man who postured like a peacock. God knew that Hollywood had enough of them anyway, and the shooting range attracted more than its fair share.

"I trust, then," Thone said in a casual voice, "that a second take won't be necessary."

Springer spread his hands before him and shook his head. "No way, dude. That was poetry in motion. The lighting was dead-on solid to catch glints off the brass as it was ejected from that rifle. We got a winner here. After I play with it a little while in the cutting room."

Thone acknowledged the compliment with a small bow that he'd learned from his Prussian grandfather. "I look forward to seeing the fruits of our labors."

"Sure. Let me get a few more interiors of the gallery, then I'll be out of your hair."

"Of course." Thone motioned to Vanessa Dearborn, the shooting gallery's manager.

Dearborn was in her late twenties and looked as if she'd spent much of that time in a gym and beauty salon. Her blond hair was shaved on the back and sides, leaving an unruly mop on the top of her head. Her violet eyes were as cosmetic as much of the enhanced figure, which was draped in a plunging emerald silk blouse and a black skirt cut daringly up the side to her hip to reveal a hint of the top of the stockings beneath.

Thone didn't like women who worshipped a plastic surgeon's knife, but Dearborn was extremely effective in her role as manager of the shooting gallery, as well as being an excellent shot.

"Vanessa," Thone said, taking her hand for a moment, "please see to it that Mr. Springer gets whatever assistance he needs in wrapping up this project."

"Yes, sir." Dearborn also knew her place, yet loved the power that came with being Thone's second in the gallery. "This way, Mr. Springer."

The young director followed her eagerly, already talking to her about the career she had in movies if she wanted one.

Thone made his way to the private office that overlooked the gallery. At least a dozen patrons stepped forward to congratulate him on his shooting. He smiled and took their hands, quickly and firmly disengaging himself from conversation.

Salvatore Mancuso waited for him in the office, a drink freshly poured and waiting on the spacious wet bar in the corner. He raised his glass in a silent toast.

"Where did you find this idiot?" Thone demanded as he crossed the room and took up the schnapps.

"He comes highly recommended."

Thone walked to the large one-way glass overlooking the shooting gallery proper. He spotted Dearborn easily, still guiding Springer and his entourage about the premises. The director was fanning out his cameramen with the tactical skill of an invading general.

"He is very good at what he does," Mancuso said. "Several big names are interested in developing some projects with him. I think we're lucky to get him for the money we could before he becomes more marketable."

Thone let his breath hiss out between his teeth. The schnapps created a warm glow in his belly and washed away some of the anger, but touched none of the frustration he'd been living with for months now.

"You just don't like him," Mancuso stated.

Thone looked at his friend and accountant. Mancuso had been with him since 1980 when he'd moved the family corporation from Germany to California, taken it from private ownership to shares for sale on Wall Street, and changed the name from Festung Armor to Fortress Arms. Over those turbulent years, the Sicilian had earned the right to speak his mind without fearing retribution.

"No," Thone agreed. "I don't like him. But he appears knowledgeable about what he's doing."

"He is. Trust me, Hayden. I've never failed you." Mancuso sipped his drink in silent contemplation of his employer. Tall and thin, the Sicilian cut an imposing figure. In his early fifties, his combed-back hair had gone silver years earlier and contrasted sharply with his dark skin. The suit he wore showed a tailor's expert hand. "These troubles we're experiencing, they'll pass in time."

"They lost half the shipment going into Canada."

"When?"

"I just found out about it a few minutes ago."

"The Russians?"

"And the Canadians and some American Justice agents from what I understand."

Mancuso took a moment to digest the information. "What about the other half?"

"It's still in transit, but I can't trust how secure that line is. The Triad has already paid half the money up front. I can't fail to deliver."

"The Canadians are still after the other half of the shipment?"

Thone nodded. "As well as the Americans."

"Can you get any more guns up there?"

"In time. I'm working on another deal for some American arms now. I'll know soon if it goes through. It might be too late by then."

"Maybe it would be in our best interests to insure the Canadians find the Triad leadership," Mancuso suggested. He spread his free hand expressively. "After all, if there are no clients who can declare foul, we would be much better off."

Thone flashed a bitter smile and shot the Sicilian with a forefinger. "You have a very devious and nasty mind, my friend."

"Thank you."

"I'll think on it." Thone glanced around the office. Behind the big teak desk that held an intercom system and a computer, rows of black-and-white and color pictures in expensive wooden frames lined the wall. Many showed Thone meeting with various heads of state, as well as the last two American presidents and representatives from the National Rifle Association.

Fortress Arms had its roots in Germany, and had survived several wars and more than four hundred years. At times, the family-owned company had commanded fortunes that rivaled the Krupp family holdings in the munitions business. He'd kept most of that history from showing up on the wall.

His grandfather would have turned over in his grave if he'd known. But the old patriarch didn't. World War II had nearly bankrupted Festung Armor. It had taken the war-torn 1960s and creative business decisions on Thone's part to keep the company afloat. Gunrunning wasn't new by any means, but he'd managed to monopolize a good section of it long enough in the late 1960s to keep the company out of the hands of its creditors and in the black.

Thone sat at the desk. "In the twenty-something years I've been this company's president, and now its CEO, there's never been a time when the wolf wasn't a stone's throw from the door."

"We're making strides," Mancuso said.

His boss took a remote control from a desk drawer, aimed it at a thirty-inch television mounted on the wall to his left and switched the set on. Colored snow erupted on the screen for a moment, then the picture cleared. The CNN signature on the feed was in a corner, and a banner proclaimed that it was being broadcast from Dover, England.

"The assassination attempt on the prime minister in England also failed," Thone said.

"A run of bad luck, Hayden. Nothing more."

Keeping the set muted, Thone said, "We're gamblers, my friend. And we've been riding a streak of bad luck of late. Every gambler, no matter how deep his pockets, can't afford to constantly be busted by the house. The Brady Bill is cutting deeply into our legitimate business enterprises."

"We no longer depend on legitimate business for our principal source of income." Mancuso retreated to the bar long enough to freshen his drink. "We have the gunrunning operations, and we have the Huntsman.''

Thone grinned in spite of the pressure he felt. "It's always good to know we have the Huntsman, and that he will always be there ready to die for us however many times we need him to. However, that brings up another sore point—they still haven't recovered the Huntsman's body from Dover.''

"They will.''

"Someone outside the conventional police agencies has it,'' Thone said.

"Who?''

"I don't know. Yet.''

Mancuso shrugged. "Even so, what will they make of it?''

"Possibly everything.''

The Sicilian waved it away. "As I've always stated, you worry too much.'' He took a seat in front of the desk and leaned forward. "We've put this plan into motion for years, Hayden. Do you really think someone can destroy it in a matter of days?''

Thone switched stations and found another news channel. The focus there appeared to be the upcoming talks in Israel between the Israeli government and radical Palestinians. "I have to ask myself whether it's solid, or whether we have just built ourselves a house of cards.''

"I'm not going to play devil's advocate. You know you feel secure in this. You've gambled everything you own to get you this far.''

"I know.''

"It'll stand,'' Mancuso said. "We built well.''

"And we buried well, too," Thone said with a grin. "Everyone who stood in our way." He sipped his drink.

"There is an additional problem." Mancuso leaned to one side and drew up an expensive briefcase. He worked the locks as he spoke. "Jacques Villon has put together a hostile takeover bid against the shares Fortress Arms has exposed on the Wall Street market."

"How?"

Mancuso shrugged. "Cash-flow problems. You know we've had those since the beginning. We needed a quick influx of cash back in August, so we put some shares out on the market. For the past few months, I've been in the process of recovering them. As we agreed." He spread some papers across the desktop.

Thone consulted them quickly, easily reading the real story behind the business and banking terms. Villon was a chief competitor of Fortress Arms these days. Villon Shooters, Inc. had put some good merchandise on the market in the past couple years, and Jacques Villon himself had gotten involved with the Hollywood crowd, catering to the gun nuts that flourished among the action-picture people.

Back in the early 1980s, Thone had made the connection with Hollywood, often supplying guns and cutlery to the movie industry free of charge for advertising purposes. One of the specially altered Colt Government Model .45s Thone had designed for one action film was still being sold to collectors. And copies of the killer's knife in a series of shock thrillers had become cult items, especially after three prostitutes in Santa Monica were discovered to have been killed by one of them. Thone had ordered the murders almost as an afterthought, and the resultant advertising and publicity had kept his name in the news for months.

Hollywood had been a good move.

Thone laid the papers on the desk. "What do you need?"

"A couple days. No more. I have the money to buy back most of the exposed shares—enough of them so that Villon's takeover bid can be quietly quashed. At the moment, I'm finding myself in a bidding war with the people who have the outstanding shares. Villon is investing heavily to get them, and cutting deeply into my bankroll. It could cause problems."

"Do Villon's people know about this?"

"Of course. How else was I supposed to find out?"

"Right. If Villon were removed from the action, would that buy you the time you needed?"

Mancuso considered that, then nodded. "I think so. His company isn't set up like ours. He's in charge of everything that goes on. Before they continued doing business, there would have to be a certain amount of restructuring done."

"You'd have the exposed shares covered by then?"

"Yes."

Thone reached for the phone and dialed. After three rings it was picked up.

"Yes?" The voice was cold and impersonal, and a hint of the Southern backwoods accent still lingered among the words.

Thone knew the call had been forwarded to the man's car phone because he could hear the hiss of tires on pavement in the background. "Lex, I have something I need you to take care of."

"Who?"

"Jacques Villon."

Thone looked at Mancuso and asked, "Where is he?" Mancuso extended a typed sheet of paper bearing a French Riviera address. The arms dealer read off the address.

"When?"

Thone knew Alexander De Moray wasn't a man to waste words. He was a stone killer who enjoyed his work. Without him, the Huntsman—in all his various incarnations—wouldn't have been possible. "Yesterday."

De Moray laughed. "If the sun went the other way, I could do that."

"Just get there as soon as you can. And let me know when it's done."

"Sure you don't want the Huntsman to do it?"

Thone grinned. "Lex, you know you're the only man I trust completely when the chips are down to kill somebody I need killed. Besides myself. And I can't be there."

"You want anything special?"

"Just kill him."

De Moray broke the connection.

Mancuso stuck a finger down his shirt collar and loosened it. He looked slightly ill. "De Moray?"

Thone nodded.

"That man makes me uncomfortable."

Laughing, Thone said, "Who the hell are you kidding? Lex scares the living shit out of you. One of these days you should sit down with him and have him tell you about his days on the CIA's Steve Canyon program in Laos. Once you get past his love of gore, some of the stories are quite entertaining."

"I don't think so."

A harsh buzz came from the intercom on one side of the desk. Thone flipped the toggle and announced himself.

"Mr. Thone, this is Cox with building security."

"Go ahead, Mr. Cox." Thone reached for the computer and switched it on, then grabbed the mouse. He shunted his way through the system and accessed the security feeds. A camera menu came up, and he waited for the guard.

"We have a disturbance at the front entrance, sir."

Thone clicked the mouse to bring up the cameras at the front of the building. Clay Pigeons, Fortress Arms's premier and exclusive shooting gallery, was located on a piece of choice real estate in Santa Monica. He'd spent millions of dollars developing the property, and it had yet to be in the black on operating costs. But it provided him a stage to meet people and do business while hiding secrets very few knew about.

The monitor cleared as the camera was activated. A crowd had gathered in the valet parking area in front of the building. They carried signs petitioning for gun control and against the NRA and Fortress Arms. A few of them were of Thone himself, armed with impossibly large guns. None of them were flattering.

Four of Thone's personal security guards stood firm ahead of the camera. They held nightsticks at the ready, grim and impersonal in their rust-red uniforms. One of the protesters threw an empty soft drink bottle at the guards. Brandishing his nightstick, a guard smashed it out of the air, sending gleaming shards spraying to catch the last rays of sunset. The street in front of the gallery had already become a river of lights flowing in both directions.

"As you can see," Cox said, "things are on the verge of getting out of control."

"Have you notified the police?"

"Yes, sir. They have a couple cars en route."

"Stay on top of the situation, Mr. Cox," Thone said with iron in his voice. "We enjoy a tenuous position here at best these days. I don't want anything physical to break out."

"I appreciate that, sir. But those men are putting their asses on the line out there."

"Understood, Mr. Cox. I didn't say they weren't to protect themselves. I just don't want us to exacerbate the situation any further."

"Yes, sir. Some of our members have already been inconvenienced by the protesters. They left just a little while ago without getting out of their cars."

Thone gazed past the milling crowd and saw two television crews from different stations setting up on the sidewalk. There was no way to keep the demonstration from getting high-profile exposure. He curbed his anger, letting it simmer, sure that he would find a place to release it later. Too many things were going wrong to think that he wouldn't have the chance to get his hands dirty at some point.

"Keep me posted, Mr. Cox." He broke the connection but continued to watch the monitor.

"They knew about the taping sequence today," Mancuso said.

"How?"

"It was advertised in the trade papers. You're news, Hayden. And when Springer was hired for the director's job, his people made sure it was mentioned in all the right places."

"This goddamned advertising had better really move some guns and knives," Thone said coldly. Since he couldn't advertise the weapons on regular programming in the United States, he'd agreed with Mancuso's plans to produce a half-hour infomercial promoting Fortress Arms's internationally manufactured weapons. The production, inflated to an hour by adding more shooting sequences with a number of actors and actresses, was also set to be rendered onto videotape for rental in video rental stores.

"It will."

Thone returned his attention to the newscast on the television. More in-depth reporting was going on covering the major constituents in the peace talks in Israel. Faces came up on the screen, some of them he'd marked for death. It would be interesting to see who survived to greet the morning.

The phone rang. He answered it mechanically, his voice as devoid of emotion as a civil servant.

"I got something else on the burner," De Moray said without preamble.

"What?"

"The head honcho of the Shivs just let me know he's not going to be able to deliver on the payment he owes us for the guns."

Thone leaned back in his chair and worked to remember who the man was they were dealing with. "Morales, right?"

"Right."

"We're supposed to be getting two hundred thousand dollars in cocaine from him in exchange for the guns."

"That's the deal."

"And now he can't come up with the dope?"

"That's what he says."

"Why?" Thone queried.

"Business is bad. They lost a couple crack houses in San Diego to vice, and one of the local biker groups, Satan's Blitz, has been kicking the shit out of them, trying to take over their turf."

"Is this true?"

"The vice raids were in the news last night. Pretty good footage. Gutsy photographer, I tell you. About the Blitz, I've heard some rumors. Personally I figure Morales has the drugs stashed somewhere and is just shining us on."

"Will he meet with us?"

De Moray laughed. It was a chilling experience. "I'm ahead of you, leader man. I got a face-to-face set up for ten o'clock tonight at Huntington Beach."

"They agreed?"

"They owe us big bucks. And Morales thinks he's smooth enough to get some more guns out of us to help him handle his problems before he pays us any heavy dinero."

"Goddamned amateurs," Thone growled. "I hate dealing with amateurs."

"My sentiments exactly. Oh, he won't come alone, but he'll believe he has the deal wired."

Thone considered the problem. He needed the money, but he'd needed the money for six weeks now. Steps had to be taken. "What time is your flight?"

"I can make the meet," De Moray said. "Gives me an hour to spare if I keep the hammer down to the airport and make a puddle-jump flight out of Laguna Beach. There's a guy I know down there who operates a charter helicopter service. It's all been arranged. That puts me at LAX for the earliest flight out for the East Coast and a straight hop to Paris from there, not counting refueling. I figured you wanted me to go commercial instead of taking one of the company jets."

"Right. Where can I meet you?"

"You want in on this?"

"Yes."

De Moray's chilling laughter filled the phone connection again. "Personal antistress program?"

"Something like that."

"It's good to see you haven't lost your taste for this kind of thing."

"Where?"

De Moray gave the name of a small restaurant and directions on how to get there.

Coolly, feeling the anticipation already welling up inside him, Thone cradled the phone and glanced back at the television screen.

"It's not wise for you to involve yourself in situations like this anymore," Mancuso observed. He steepled his fingers before him and peered over them. "You're a legitimate businessman."

Thone grinned. "Only on a superficial level. And so are you. I've never met anyone who could cook books the way you do." He closed a hand and made a fist that rapped against the desktop. "These people are screwing me around, Sal, and an example needs to be set. Back in 1968, my father was killed by a group of freedom fighters he was supplying to fight against the Russians. That's *not* going to happen to me."

"Then, be careful."

"I'll have Lex with me. If there ever was a more efficient killing machine, I've not seen its like."

A splash of magenta suddenly washed across the computer monitor.

Leaning forward, Thone tapped a button. The screen cleared, revealing the fight that had broken out in front of Clay Pigeons. The group of protesters swung their signs with enthusiasm, pushing their front line up against the shooting gallery's defenders. The security guards used their batons vigorously, beating the aggressors back. In the background, three police cars came to an abrupt halt, strangely silent because the camera didn't have an audio pickup.

"Damn," Thone said. "Get in touch with someone in public relations and have them handle this with the media. And get our attorneys working on it, too. I want to know if there's anyone we can hold responsible for this bullshit."

Mancuso reached for the phone. "Where are you going to be?"

Thone stood and pressed a hidden button behind one of the pictures on the wall. A section of the wall slid away, revealing an armory of weapons in a secret niche. The inventory ran from pistols to rifles to knives. A SEAL crossbow hung on the right along with a hip quiver of bolts. After only a moment's contemplation, he selected an H&K VP-70 Z. After checking the action and finding it fully loaded, he opened one of the drawers below the wall of guns and chose a shoulder rig that would fit the pistol. "Unavailable for comment. As far as the media is to know, I've not even been made aware of the events here."

Mancuso talked to someone in the public-relations office and quickly outlined what had happened.

Stripping off his jacket, Thone shrugged into the shoulder holster and thrust the gun home. When the accountant got off the phone, he said, "Keep me apprised of what's going on in Canada. I'm going to send a team into the area to prevent losing the other half of the Russian arms shipment."

Mancuso nodded.

Looking forward to the meet on the beach despite the probable loss of income, Thone walked to the east end of the office. He moved the heat and air-conditioning levers on the climate control. A hidden door opened and he passed through. The gallery had a level beneath it that even most of the employees didn't know about. He was sure he could get out of the building undetected. When he thought about Morales, the weight of the gun in his shoulder holster made him smile. Despite his managerial capacity in Fortress Arms, he knew he was a lot like his grandfather: he liked to get his hands dirty in the business. When he reached the midnight blue Mercedes 540SL, he was whistling a Louis Prima jazz number. Notwithstanding the problems he had, Thone felt life was pretty good.

**7**

"Surely there's someone else you can get to do this," Brognola said.

"Of course there is, Hal," the President of the United States replied agreeably. "But cutting to the bottom line, I want you to do this."

Brognola stared through the bug-splattered windshield of his car and shifted the mobile phone on his shoulder while he fumbled for a cigar from his jacket pocket. The light at the intersection turned green, and he slipped into the flow of late-night Washington, D.C., traffic. "The Stony Man teams are involved in some heavy-hitting affairs across the board now."

"I'm aware of that," the Man stated. "But Barbara Price is quite capable of handling those missions."

"Yeah, but I just don't like being out of touch with so much going on."

"There's never a quiet time for your group. We both know that. And I need this taken care of. There's no one else I'd rather see at the helm. We're dealing with a number of international agencies on this. I don't want the main thrust of this getting blunted by petty bureaucratic jealousies."

Brognola shifted the unlighted cigar to the side of his mouth and took out a package of antacid tablets. He shook two out in his hand, then reconsidered and added a third. There was still the Treasury guy, Walton, to go through tonight. He crunched the tablets and swallowed hopefully. His stomach had been rolling since the conversation had started.

"When do I need to be in Miami?" the big Fed asked.

"They're expecting you tomorrow morning. Special Agent Walton will brief you on the specifics."

Brognola made a turn at the light. "If you don't mind my saying so, sir, the Treasury Department's probably a lot more schooled in counterfeiting rings than I am. I worked a few cases in bunco coming up through the ranks, but nothing that would really shed any light on this."

"Talk to Walton," the President suggested. "My nose tells me there's more to this than simple counterfeiting. You talk to Walton and spend a couple days down in Miami, and if you don't get the same feeling, I'll front you first class tickets to bring you home."

"That's the best deal I can cut?"

"That's the only deal on the table, Hal." The President hesitated. "Don't get me wrong. I'm not just acting as your boss here, I'm asking for your help, too."

"All right. I'll take a look. As soon as I know something, you'll know it."

The President broke the connection.

Shifting in his seat, Brognola tried to get comfortable. He checked the streets again at the next light and made another turn, sliding off Connecticut Avenue onto the side street he was looking for. The area was known to native Washingtonians as the 19th Street Corridor, running north from Pennsylvania Avenue to the Dupont Circle. He'd been there a number of times before. The area was frequented by office people looking for respite from the nine-to-five grind.

He located the comedy club without problem and found a place in back in the graveled parking lot. Judging from the number of cars present, the club did a healthy business. He retrieved his Chief's Special and an extra speed-loader from the glove compartment and got out. Out of habit, he checked to see if anyone was paying extraordinary attention to him while he worked the key ring. Satisfied that he had gone relatively unnoticed, he leathered the pistol in the paddle holster at his right side, dropped the speed-loader in his jacket pocket, then locked the car.

The front of the club was lighted up with a flashing marquee advertising KIMBER'S KOMEDY KARO-SEL. Spray-can art covered the brickwork, depicting a variety of comic actors and actresses.

Brognola paid for a ticket and was told that the show was already ten minutes in progress. After assuring the guy he was there more to meet a friend than to take in a whole night of comedy, he was ushered through the doors.

The interior of the club was small, almost intimate. Cigarette smoke helped cloud the darkness already settled into the room. A spotlight filtered through the blue haze and landed on a male comedian dressed in jeans, a black T-shirt and wraparound sunglasses. He had a cigarette in one hand and a drink in the other as he worked his routine.

Eyes adjusting to the dimness, Brognola made out Glen Walton as the Treasury agent spotted him and waved him over to a small round table. The big Fed crossed the tightly packed floor with aid from a small brunette working the tables.

"I was beginning to wonder if you were going to make it," Walton said.

Brognola took a seat on the bar stool. "Got tied up in traffic."

Walton nodded. The Treasury agent was compactly built, young, and already had thinning hair that was made even more pronounced by the short style he wore. Reflected light gleamed from his watch and ring as he lifted a beer bottle and drank deeply. His eyes were hooded by the shadows, but roved constantly. "My boss heard you weren't overly fond of this assignment."

"You know how rumor goes around in this town."

"Yeah. But Treasury should have gotten the tag on this one."

Brognola didn't try to debate the issue. He was holding all of the cards and both of them knew it. Otherwise the younger man wouldn't have been there. The waitress came by and the head Fed ordered decaf coffee.

Walton raised the empty beer bottle. "Officially I'm off duty."

"Look, son, I'm not going to be anywhere near your next quarterly review, so let's skip the bid for heading off any recriminations." The waitress returned with the coffee, left it and went on her way. Brognola raised the steaming cup. "Officially I catch the next red-eye out of town and I don't sleep so good on the damn plane. Now let's see what you've got.''

Talk was prohibited by the sound system and the gales of laughter from the crowd. The comedian, wreathed in cigarette smoke, was hitting his stride.

Walton passed over a thick folder. ''It'll take you some time to get through all of it. Give you something to do on the plane.''

Opening the folder, Brognola flipped through the contents. The light was bad in the club but was good enough that he could make out a few of the details of the pictures. At least a dozen hundred-dollar bills were included, mounted on pasteboard behind protective plastic sheets. Captions beneath each bill gave a brief history of where and when it was recovered. The ones Brognola glanced at covered an eight-month time frame.

There were other pictures of individuals who'd been previously arrested for counterfeiting in North America. All of them appeared to be suspects in the case.

Brognola closed the folder, then took a rubber band from his pocket and bound it together. ''Pretty extensive,'' he commented.

''We've got some time in on this deal,'' Walton said. ''That's why it chafes everybody's ass that you were called in.''

Ignoring the observation, the head Fed asked, ''Who have you come up with?''

''There's a number of possibilities,'' Walton admitted. ''We've narrowed down the scope of the search, but you're still looking at more than two-dozen possibles in there. Those are good bills. We didn't discover them easily, and it was more luck than anything else. They've got different serial numbers, a lot of them, and they don't usually show up in any one area too often. They've also got good paper stock.''

''One source or many?''

The waitress dropped off a fresh beer and Walton sipped. ''We're not sure. If it is one source, the operation is tied in like you wouldn't believe. These bills are turning up all over the world.''

''Yeah,'' Brognola said, ''that's what I was told. Interpol and other foreign police agencies are gathering in Miami to form a clearing house for all the information everyone's accumulated. Supposed to cut down on the duplication of manpower and give us a better picture of what's going on.''

''Right now the Japanese hate us, and the Europeans aren't too crazy about us, either.'' Walton shifted in his seat and started peeling the label from his beer bottle. ''All those countries use American money due to tourism. They took some pretty big hits when the counterfeit stuff was discovered. Screwed up international trade balances something fierce behind closed doors.''

''How much is out there?''

''God only knows, because we sure as hell don't. Conservative estimates range anywhere from one hundred million dollars to a billion. Our guys think even more than that is out there.''

Brognola let that sink in. The Man hadn't mentioned actual figures, just said that the problem was staggering.

''Counterfeit has always been a problem,'' Walton went on. ''But there's never been enough of it out there to damage us financially. There have been counterfeit bills floating through everyday money exchanges for years. Usually twenties because they don't attract as much attention. But business has gotten bigger and the demand for liquid cash has, too. Hundred-dollar bills are more prevalent than they used to be. Little girls working the registers at fast-food joints are starting to cash them and not make a big deal out of it."

"When I was coming up through the ranks," Brognola said, "counterfeit was just a con man's game. A guy could make a few bucks at it over a period of time, or he could pass it off to someone else working a crooked deal and hope he didn't get killed for his trouble."

"This leaves those days in the shade. There's enough funny money out there to seriously damage our economy here, and hurt our standing in several foreign countries. The reason for the meet down in Miami is that all their top guys have agreed that the U.S. is the one with the leak. They're not really here to compare notes. If they were able to pull all the counterfeit out of the cash flow, there'd be holes in the economy that you could drive government budgets through. But they can't let the money keep hitting the streets. They want to plug the dam, however they have to."

Brognola reached for another couple antacid tablets. The Treasury agent's words left his stomach sour. Not only was he going to have to play bureaucrat to the hilt in Miami, but he was going to be doing it over a gang of legal and diplomatically immune headhunters looking for shortcuts.

A crooked grin twisted Walton's lips. "Actually, with that said, maybe I'm glad we're only involved peripherally now."

Glancing at his watch, Brognola found it was after eleven. His plane was scheduled to leave shortly before midnight. He gathered the folder and drained the coffee cup. He reached into his wallet and left a tip.

"I'll walk you out," Walton said. He checked the bill and dropped money on the table.

Brognola fell in behind the man, and they made their way through the exit door. The big Fed felt relieved to be out in the night air and sucked it down gratefully.

Walton paused to light a cigarette. "Where are you parked?"

Brognola pointed.

"You know, I picked this club for our meet because my superiors at the Treasury Department have been picking up some indications of outside interest on this investigation. They weren't really forthcoming with the information, but I've learned how to read the signs."

Out of the corner of his eye, Brognola noticed the exit door open behind them.

Walton didn't break stride, but his hand drifted down for the gun belted on his hip. "I figured we meet in a place like the comedy club where the crowd didn't generally leave until a preset time, we'd notice anyone interested in us."

"You were tailed."

"Looks that way," Walton agreed.

Three men stepped out of the club dressed in dark street clothes. Two of them were white, the third man black.

"Of course," the Treasury agent said, "the show was pretty bad. Those guys could just be realizing they've wasted some money."

Without warning, lights flared to life in front of Brognola. The big Fed identified them as belonging to an older Cadillac just as the Detroit dinosaur surged out of the parking space, spraying gravel from under the tires to smash against the hurricane fence surrounding the lot.

Fisting the Chief's .38 from his hip, Brognola shouted a warning and dodged to the left.

A gunner with a machine pistol leaned out the passenger-side window. A dozen miniature suns dawned in the gunner's hands and the roar of autofire echoed through the lot. Bullets smashed against loose gravel and sent rocks flying. Another burst ripped the hubcap from a nearby Chevy El Camino and deflated the tire.

Brognola rolled the hammer back on the .38 and put a round squarely through the driver's side of the windshield. He took cover behind the El Camino as a line of .45 rounds cut through the bodywork. Thumbing the hammer back again, he took deliberate aim on the gunner, then fired. The .38 hollowpoint took the man in the top of the skull and destroyed all motor control.

Desperately the driver cut the wheel and floored the accelerator. The Caddie slammed into the lighter El Camino and shoved the car forward.

Brognola backpedaled, struggling to stay out of the way of the tons of metal sliding toward him. Harsh screeches drowned out all the street sounds, punctuated by the booming reports of Walton's pistol somewhere off to the right. He slammed up against the hurricane fence, cushioning the impact with his left arm and feeling it go numb from the elbow down.

The Caddy's driver put the transmission in reverse and tried to pull away.

Shifting sideways, Brognola dropped the .38 into target acquisition and forgot about the pistol's sights, concentrating on his quarry. He squeezed the last three rounds through in double-action as quick as he could.

The windshield fragmented, and the driver slumped behind the wheel an instant before the Cadillac thudded into the comedy club.

Making his arm work in spite of the numbness, Brognola flipped the .38's cylinder open and shook out the empty brass. They tinkled when they struck the gravel between the head Fed's feet, and the sound—so unexpected and clear—made him realize how much he'd locked his senses on the threat of the vehicle.

Brognola spun, flipping the cylinder expertly closed and easing back the hammer as he glanced around for Walton. The Treasury agent was holding his own against two men firing from cover around the club's exit doors. Two other gunners lay sprawled across the pavement leading to the graveled lot.

Sirens screamed in the distance.

Walton fired from a two-handed Weaver stance. His bullets chopped through the open storm door one man was crouched behind and chased the guy into a break for a nearby car.

Brognola took a bead on the second gunner and dropped the hammer. The .38 hollowpoint caught the man in the chest and knocked him backward. The loose manner in which he collapsed to the ground told the big Fed that the man wouldn't be getting back up.

Walton dropped an empty clip from his 10 mm Colt Delta Elite and shoved home a fresh one. His first three bullets picked up the other gunner as the guy broke for more distant cover and dropped him in a writhing tangle of arms and legs.

"Get back inside the club, damn it!" Brognola roared at the curious spectators who had gathered at the door. "Call 911!"

There was a moment of hesitation, then the heads retreated.

Brognola knew from the sounds of the sirens that law-enforcement teams were already on the way. He reached into his pocket and retrieved a flip phone. He extended the antenna. Punching with one hand while he approached the stalled Cadillac with Walton closing the distance behind him, he got through to the Washington, D.C., police department's main switchboard. He quickly identified himself and the situation, giving the location and the fact that two federal agents were on the scene in civilian clothes. The switchboard operator relayed the information to the homicide cop who'd assumed command of the site. Satisfied, Brognola put the flip phone away.

The Cadillac's engine ticked as it cooled. Nothing moved beyond the car's sea of broken glass.

With his left hand supporting his right wrist, Brognola held the .38 on the car as he advanced slowly. Walton was to his left.

"I got the door," Brognola said.

"I got your back."

The big Fed put his hand on the door handle and yanked it open. A dead man slipped out, his upper chest ruined by bullets. Broken glass glinted in the wounds.

The guy in the passenger seat was dead, as well, but the man in the rear seat was merely unconscious, a great gash ripped across his forehead to his left ear. White bone shone through the wound, but Brognola believed the man would live.

"You know any of these guys?" the big Fed asked.

Relaxing his hold on the pistol but keeping it accessible, Walton shook his head. "Not any players I've ever seen."

"Me neither." Brognola kept the Treasury agent covered as he pulled the unconscious man from the Cadillac. The first patrol car screeched to a wary halt out in the street, and a searchlight flared over the parking lot as Walton secured the prisoner's hands behind his back with metal handcuffs.

A shadow ran from the passenger side of the patrol car and took up a flanking position near the entrance to the parking lot. Overhead, a police chopper drifted into view, then stabbed a beam of harsh white light over the parked cars until it washed over Brognola and held steady. An unmarked sedan rolled to a controlled halt in the street, then nosed toward the parking lot. A whirling blue cherry sat on the driver's side of the rooftop.

"Got four guys at the back with riot guns," Walton said quietly.

"I guess they took this call pretty seriously."

"No shit."

The unmarked car braked less than ten feet away. A massive black man in a trench coat and sharply creased fedora climbed out from behind the steering wheel. An equally massive blue-steel S&W Model 29 .44 Magnum filled his right fist. "I'm looking for a guy named Brognola," he said in a voice that inspired penitence.

"Me," the big Fed replied.

"Some ID?"

Brognola reached for his inside jacket pocket. The black man made no effort to approach. "You see it from there?"

"No, but I got a guy with a scope out there in that car who can. You just be real still." Brognola opened his wallet and held it steady.

"Checks out," the guy in the squad car yelled.

"You Rollie Maurloe?" Brognola asked, putting his wallet away.

"The same." The homicide detective walked forward but didn't put his pistol away. "Any of them left alive?"

"One. Here."

"Who's the guy with you?"

"Special Agent Glen Walton of the Treasury Department." Brognola remembered where he'd heard Maurloe's name before. Able Team had bumped into the homicide detective a few times and managed a working relationship with the man while maintaining a low profile on their operations.

A wide grin split Maurloe's face. "Been wanting to meet you for some time, Brognola. I've had a few run-ins with some pretty rowdy boys you handle."

Brognola put his pistol away and took out a cigar. "Yeah."

"Are you here?" the homicide detective asked.

Brognola grinned slightly and shook his head. "I'm smoke."

"So I can't touch you?"

"Nope."

Maurloe shifted his eyes to Walton. "What about this joker?"

"Not mine."

"Well, now, he'll be mine for a while, then. I got a lot of bodies around here that need explaining, and it just gladdens my poor old heart that I've got someone to talk to about it."

Walton glanced at Brognola. "Thanks a lot."

"Give him some of it," the big Fed replied. "He's salt of the earth where cop work is concerned. He knows how to keep his mouth shut."

"Yeah, but he's a homicide dick. He's not even going to start believing me until the third or fourth repetition."

"And the rubber hoses," Maurloe said enthusiastically. "Don't forget the rubber hoses."

"You learned some new jokes tonight," Brognola said. "It should keep the both of you entertained."

"Terrific," Walton snarled.

"You shoot anybody here tonight?" Maurloe asked Brognola.

"Yeah."

"You got an extra piece?"

Brognola nodded. There was a .357 Magnum under the driver's seat of his car.

"If you let me have that one," Maurloe said, "it'll be easier to put a bow on things here."

Brognola handed over the pistol.

Maurloe took it, then wiped the prints off with a handkerchief. He stuck it out at the Treasury agent butt first. "Here."

"So I killed them all?" Walton asked.

"Sure," Maurloe said with a shrug. "Why not? The way I'll tell it, you're a regular goddamned Two-Gun Kid. Your people hear about it, I bet you don't have to qualify for your next shooting review."

Walton took the pistol, then handed it back. Maurloe dropped it in a coat pocket.

Brognola turned and walked toward his car as the police ring tightened and started to drive back the gathering crowd.

"Hey, Brognola," Walton called.

The big Fed halted for a moment.

"You keep your head down while you're in the Sunshine State. These guys got a hard-on like this for you, they aren't going to stop after one failed hit."

Brognola nodded, then glanced at Maurloe. "I'll be in touch for whatever information you turn up on these people."

The big homicide detective turned a palm up. "When you get where you're going, and you turn up something that'll help me straighten out the kinks you're leaving me with here . . ."

"I'll drop a quarter."

"Fair enough."

Brognola got in his car and pulled out of the parking lot. A glance at his watch let him know he'd have to hustle to make his flight. He lifted the phone and

placed a call to Price at Stony Man Farm. There was
no telling what was waiting for him at Miami, and he
intended to shave the odds in his favor as much as
possible.

**8**

"I take it you're not worried about collecting the money?"

Hayden Thone looked at Alexander De Moray.

In the pale moonlight spilling over the beachfront and reflecting from the rolling gentle waves, the man looked positively elemental. His hair was a thick shock of unruly black that fell across his broad forehead and emphasized his pallid complexion that was evidence of his nocturnal life-style. Although at six feet three and carrying more than two hundred pounds of lean, corded muscle, De Moray gave the impression of quiet control and reserve. He wore sunglasses even at night, lending him an insectoid and alien gaze. The black duster he wore swirled restlessly in the breeze coming in off the ocean. His black jeans were neatly pressed, and the pant legs were tucked into the calf-high black Wellington hiking boots. He reached into the pocket of his black silk shirt and brought out a package of cigarettes.

"No," Thone answered. "The money is no longer the issue here."

"So you figure on showing Morales's people you can play hardball?" De Moray shook out a cigarette and flipped open his lighter with a metallic ping. He never broke stride, cupping the wavering yellow-and-orange flame between his palms. In the glow, his perfect features looked cold and artificial, and the Vietnamese beer bottle cap mounted on the lighter's side gleamed.

"Hardly. That wouldn't solve anything." Thone pulled his jacket on a little more tightly, checking the weight of the H&K VP-70 Z in shoulder leather. "If we arrange a promotion for the next man under Morales, I figure that during the reorganization we should find someone more predisposed to do business properly with us."

"Always the businessman."

Thone's feet made chuffing noises as he walked across the loose sand. "Always the professional. Business is as much a profession as killing."

"Yeah, but I get to the bottom line quicker." De Moray chuckled coldly. He glanced ahead. "Look alive, the other guests just made the party."

Thone looked ahead, barely able to make out the three figures walking toward them. De Moray's senses bordered on the supernatural. Even with his perfect vision, Fortress Arms' CEO couldn't make out the shadows hovering near the waterline. "You're sure it's them?"

"Oh, yeah. Morales is carrying. You can tell because his hand never gets far from his left coat pocket. He's left-handed and thinks that gives him an edge because the other guy's generally watching his right hand. He also likes to shoot people through the jacket pocket. The guy with him on the right? That's Diego. You can tell by the limp. The last one is Jesus Santiago, a gunner."

Thone couldn't tell which was which. The distance dropped to something less than fifty feet, and the details sorted themselves out. Morales was coming up facing him, his hand already dropped into his jacket pocket.

At his left, De Moray had picked up the earphone that had been dangling over his shoulder and inserted it in his ear. A moment later he said, "There's five more men involved."

"Where?"

De Moray nodded at the line of wooded hills overlooking the beach. "Three up there, and two more are in a powerboat on the ocean. Four hundred yards away. Figure a couple long guns and the waves won't be that much of a problem coming in slow the way they are."

"I wouldn't miss."

"Nope. Neither would I."

"How many men do you have watching over us?"

"Two."

Thone unbuttoned his jacket and relaxed his arms at his sides. The distance had dropped to thirty feet and the approach had slowed. Sparing a glance out toward the ocean, he caught a glimpse of the powerboat's running lights. "Is the boat going to be a problem?"

"I got it covered. You just work on staying alive when Morales tries to cowboy his way out of this." A warped piece of driftwood almost four feet long and two inches thick at the widest end lay on the beach in front of De Moray. The man leaned down and picked it up with no apparent effort, then used it like a walking stick. A generous grin was on his lips as he looked at the three Shiv members.

"Hey, man," Morales called out as they came to a halt less than ten feet away. The Shiv leader was dressed in a faded jean jacket cut poncho-style, stained blue jeans and motorcycle boots decorated with small-linked chains. A bright red scarf was tied around his head. His face was a dark-skinned oval marred by a stringy mustache and a chin tuft of whiskers.

Diego was ten years older, twenty pounds too heavy, and dressed in slacks and an oxford shirt under a light cotton jacket. Santiago was all denim, chains and attitude. He openly carried a Magnum revolver in the front of his jeans. Moonlight glinted from the chain connecting his left earring with the silver stud piercing his left nostril.

Thone didn't mince words. "You owe me money." His voice was as cold as ice.

Morales made a dismissive gesture and tried a little-boy smile. He turned his right hand palm up. "I know, man. Your arm here has let me know that. I told him what's been up with my territory. Maybe he hasn't told you."

Thone smiled back, his eyes never leaving the gangbanger's. "My friend knows how little I care for bullshit."

Shaking his head as if in disbelief, Morales said, "Man, those are some harsh words. Harsh. They shouldn't belong in a conversation with two people who trust each other."

"I agree." Thone crossed his hands at his waist, his right hand inside the left. "When do I get my cocaine?"

"Soon." Morales put an edge in his voice.

"Soon," Thone repeated. "If I looked for that on a calendar, when would I find it?"

Anger knotting his jawline, Morales thrust a blunt forefinger in Thone's direction. "Look, homes, you're lucky I'm even doing business with you. There's a million guys out there willing to sell me guns."

"Maybe they can afford the loss," the Fortress Arms CEO interrupted. "I can't."

"Two hundred Gs of blow," Morales responded. "Man, it would take you weeks to turn that much shit around."

"I had a buyer. But now I'm six weeks behind and looking to find someone else to do business with. You've already cost me money."

Morales glanced at De Moray. "You want to tell this white-bread bastard the real score? Son of a bitch is so wrapped up in the economics of life that he don't realize its complexities."

"Complexities," De Moray said. "Somebody teach you a new word, Morales? You been watching *Jeopardy* again when the home boys haven't been around?"

Morales's face hardened. "Man, I got guns on you. I got guns on you this very minute. You don't walk off this beach unless I say it's okay for you to drag your asses away."

"I'll keep that in mind," De Moray said.

"Lex." Thone addressed De Moray but didn't take his eyes away from the gangbanger leader.

"Yeah?"

"This piece of shit with legs that doesn't know how to pay his bills on time?"

"Yeah?"

"If he gets wasted, does Diego inherit the gang?"

Diego's face was covered with perspiration, and he blinked rapidly. Beside him, Santiago shifted slightly, letting his hand drift closer to the butt of his revolver.

"No," De Moray answered. "Guy named Marenco does. But Diego can carry a message."

"Can we deal with Marenco?"

"I think so," De Moray replied evenly. "From the looks of things, we damn sure can't do any worse."

"You assholes are dead meat!" Morales shouted. "If I need any more guns, I'll get them somewhere else." He thrust his hand inside his jacket pocket and swung around almost into profile. Something hard and blunt pressed against the fabric of the jacket.

"Tango," De Moray said loudly so the walkie-talkie would pick him up. "You have your targets. Take them down." He went into action, raising the long piece of driftwood and ramming it into Santiago's face as the gangbanger brought the gun out of his pants. A wet, meaty noise sounded when the splintered end of the driftwood penetrated Santiago's right eye and slid through the orbital socket into the brain behind.

Moving fluidly, Thone stepped outside the swinging arm and captured the jacket-encased wrist with his left hand. He yanked down on the gangbanger's forearm. The jacket material ripped, then came apart with an explosion of sound and flash. The bullet plowed into the loose sand at their feet.

Thone freed the H&K VP-70 Z from his shoulder holster. Morales struggled to get away and flailed at Thone with his free arm. Controlling the gangbanger's efforts to get free, the head of Fortress Arms stepped into the man and kept him off balance. He leveled the 9 mm pistol under Morales's chin and pulled the trigger three times in quick succession. The reports were muffled by flesh, then buried completely by the sound of high-powered rifles and helicopter rotors.

Thone released the dead man he held and glanced up.

A Bell UH-1D cruised by overhead like a predatory shark, moving thunder illuminated by running lights. A rocket pod hung out from the right side. The pod belched as a warhead took flight, streaking toward the powerboat in the distance where muzzle flashes winked at the railing. A white vapor trail scarred the night-black sky. An instant later the rocket struck the powerboat and reduced it to scrap and flames that rained over the ocean surface.

The harsh cracks of heavy-caliber rifle fire rolled over Thone. He glanced toward the wooded hills overlooking the beachfront.

As the last of the rifle reports echoed and faded, a body tumbled from hiding and came to a sliding stop at the foot of the hills. Another had already tumbled to a halt.

"That's all three," De Moray said, holding a pair of infrared binoculars to his eyes. "The other one's still in the trees, but he's already spent the rest of his life."

Thone leathered his pistol and stepped up to Diego. The smaller man was shivering, batting his eyes wildly. Leaning forward, the CEO of Fortress Arms deliberately invaded the gangbanger's space and stripped away whatever shreds of security might be remaining. "You can take a message for me?"

There was hesitation, as if Diego hadn't realized he could move. "Yes."

"Tell Marenco I want the cocaine in three days' time, or I'm going to send my friend after him."

"I will."

"Get going," Thone ordered. "I don't want you picked up by the police or coast-guard people who come to investigate this."

Diego turned and tried to step quickly away, moving stiffly because his shoulders wouldn't loosen up, obviously expecting a bullet. Near the woodline, he finally got a full head of steam up and made a run for it.

"Man's properly motivated," De Moray commented, then chuckled.

Thone glanced up at the helicopter hovering in the distance. "Air coverage. That was a nice touch."

De Moray shook out a fresh cigarette and lighted it. The flame chiseled shadows into his lean face. "I thought so."

"You could have told me."

De Moray gazed at him speculatively. "I could have. But you came out here for an adrenaline rush. There wasn't any sense in your missing out on every opportunity." He flicked ashes onto Morales's body. "Good to see you haven't lost your stomach for the close-up work."

"There's a certain satisfaction to this business that you don't find in the boardroom."

A smile filled with feline cruelty lifted De Moray's lips. "Don't forget to get rid of that piece."

Thone shook his head and adjusted his jacket.

"Shame you have to get rid of it." De Moray reached out and pulled the piece of driftwood from the dead man's eye socket. It gleamed with dark wetness. "If you took advantage of what nature has provided, you could keep it."

"Lex, a gun to me is like Doritos to Jay Leno. If I use them, I'll toss them and make more."

"Right."

"You've got a plane to catch."

De Moray pointed toward the helicopter. A silhouette hung on to the landing skids, working on the rocket pod. As Thone watched, the pod dropped free of the chopper and splashed into the ocean. "That's my ride. Give you a lift back to your car?"

"No. You need to get started. If Villon is allowed to carry out his plans, I'll be mired in red tape for weeks. I don't need a microscope going over everything we're doing right now."

The helicopter descended to the beach and threw out clouds of sand that quickly started to cover the bodies. Two men dressed in black burst free of the shadows. De Moray waved them toward the chopper.

"You want Villon's ears?" De Moray asked.

"No. The fewer questions asked about Villon's death, the better." Even after all these years, Thone still had a hard time knowing when the other man was joking.

De Moray flipped him a sharp salute, then ran to join his crew in the aircraft.

Thone moved into a jog, running easily even in the loose sand as the helicopter lifted and vanished into the sky. He'd never neglected his physical conditioning, and the effort came naturally. When he reached his rented vehicle three minutes later, he wasn't even breathing hard. He set the radio tuner to a big-band station and tried to puzzle out what he was going to do about Brognola. He hadn't counted on the Justice agent still being alive. It would confuse what he had set up in Miami. Still, he had confidence in his resources. And there was always the Huntsman.

**9**

"They're in motion, mate."

Yakov Katzenelenbogen glanced toward the eastern sky hanging over Jerusalem. Dawn was still hours away. The Phoenix Force leader adjusted the earthroat set. David McCarter's position was south of the Hebrew Union College, providing him a clear view of the route the entourage of the American, European and Japanese negotiators was using in its approach to the King David Hotel, where the group would be staying.

Katz tapped the headset's transmit button. "Calvin?"

"I've got them" came the calm reply.

Shifting in the passenger seat of the van parked in front of the YMCA building across the street from the hotel, Katz leaned forward and stabbed out his cigarette in the ashtray. Rafael Encizo sat behind the van's steering wheel with a cellular phone in his hand. "Call them and tell them," Katz said.

The wiry Cuban dialed.

Katz wore a black beret, a dark blue turtleneck, charcoal-colored slacks and a corduroy jacket, which made him seem like a tourist. His right hand was a hooked prosthesis that replaced the flesh and blood hand lost in the Six-Day War. The Phoenix Force commander had lived in Israel for a time, had loved and fathered a family, and lost a son in one of the interminable wars that ripped through the Middle East. Finding a lasting peace between Israel and all Palestinians was important to him, and he took this security duty seriously.

He'd also been a member of the Mossad, which put him on good terms with the group they had joined forces with this night. He switched frequencies on the headset. "Ranon?"

"I am here, old friend."

"You've noticed the caravan now has a tail?"

"Of course. I've already briefed my men, but since the Americans saw fit to place you in charge of this exercise, I've been waiting for you." Ranon Goldberg was a Mossad chief and an old friend, a struggling hard-liner who saw conceding more land to the Palestinian radicals who demanded it as tantamount to opening the barn doors yet again to starving wolves. Judging from reaction in Israel, he wasn't alone in his thoughts.

"We'll proceed with some caution at first," Katz said.

"You know how to deal with these people, Yakov," Goldberg said with a touch of irritability. "When you find a snake, you cut its head off and let it die."

"Not when its thrashings could possibly bring down whole buildings. We'll test their resistance for the moment." Katz nodded at Encizo.

The Cuban keyed the ignition and pulled the van smoothly out into the sparse flow of traffic.

Katz reached under his jacket and unsnapped the SIG-Sauer P-226 sheathed under his right arm. He laid his hand on the Calico machine pistol in restraining brackets mounted on the dash, then telescoped the collapsible butt stock. The 100-round magazine mounted atop the Calico resembled a flashlight. He unfastened the seat belt so he could move out of the vehicle quickly if there was a need.

Lights from approaching cars splashed over the dirty windshield and grayed out.

"Gary," Katz called out.

Gary Manning was the team's demolitions expert, an artist with explosives and a dangerous man in any situation. "Go," the big Canadian responded softly.

"Your end of things?"

"Clean and green. You say the word, these guys get a treatment that heavy-metal concert junkies only dream about."

"Ready," Encizo whispered.

"What about you, Calvin?" Katz asked.

"Clear field of fire," the ex-SEAL replied. He was at the top of the 150-foot Oriental tower striking up from the YMCA building. Besides being the team's medic and chemist, Calvin James was also an excellent sniper. At present he was in charge of the Mossad sniping unit that would provide coverage for the counterterrorist play taking shape in the streets. "Make your contact. Your back is covered."

"I'm closing the back door," McCarter transmitted. "That's the lot of them."

"How many?"

"Four cars and two delivery trucks. You pick a number and I'll swear to it. The way they're positioning the trucks, it's a safe bet that they've got some heavy artillery tucked away there.'' David McCarter was ex-SAS. A professional soldier with a Sandhurst education, the fox-faced Briton was deadly once in the trenches.

"Affirmative," Katz said, then left the channel clear.

"There," Encizo said, pointing with his chin as he kept both hands on the wheel.

Katz looked at the oncoming traffic and saw the convoy headed for the King David Hotel. A deep maroon Mercedes limousine was in the lead, followed by a cream-colored Lincoln Continental. The Israeli knew that the American and European contingent were in the Mercedes, while the Japanese representatives trailed in the Lincoln.

Even though the first Israeli-Palestinian peace talks had been successful and the Gaza Strip and Jericho were now in Palestinian hands, one group of Islamic fundamentalists had deemed it not enough. The Palestinian Anvil of God demanded more land, and threatened to back up its claim with acts of terrorism.

Working through the Mossad intelligence network and incorporating the information Kurtzman was able to access from Stony Man Farm, Katz and his unit had learned of Anvil of God's plans to kill the international negotiators from the U.S., Europe and Japan. The obvious targets, including Arafat, who the terrorists thought had sold them out, had been placed under heavy security. If the foreign peacemakers could be killed or maimed, Anvil of God's warped thinking was that the Western countries and Japan would withdraw their interest, and leave Israel and "Palestine" to hammer out a new agreement of their own.

Phoenix Force and the Mossad contingent assigned to them were there to prevent the assassinations. Security at Ben-Gurion airport in Tel Aviv had been tight, as well as the train ride into Jerusalem. The King David Hotel had of late become a veritable fortress. The only weak link in the transportation was in the streets.

The limousine and the Lincoln passed, trailed almost immediately by one of the suspect delivery trucks. The canvas tarp billowed over the metal ribs underneath, held in place by tie-downs. Three men were on the other side of the windshield.

Katz accessed the headset. "Okay, Gary, let's build in some space."

"I'm on it," Manning replied.

"Calvin." Katz freed the Calico and flipped off the safety. Two extra 50-round magazines hung at his thigh in a modified quiver.

"Once they hit the street," James promised, "they're ours."

Katz looked at the approaching truck and nodded to Encizo. "Get it done." Then he tapped the headset button. "Go, Gary."

Encizo cut the steering wheel viciously, pulling in front of the oncoming truck. The driver gestured angrily through the open window as he braked sharply. The van slid to a halt sideways in the road.

Opening the door, Katz leaped out and landed on his feet. The Calico's barrel came to a rest across the wrist of his prosthesis. "Out of the truck and facedown on the ground!" he bellowed in Hebrew, then repeated the order in Arabic. The echoes of the verbal blast rolled over the street. The few people out around the deserted shops took cover. Even the tourists were fairly quick in their reaction time.

The passenger door of the lead truck jerked open as a man vaulted from the cab, submachine gun up and ready.

Without hesitation, Katz pulled the Calico on-line and loosed a long burst. The 9 mm rounds cored through the open truck door and caught the terrorist in full flight, punching him to the ground.

"Phoenix One, this is Stony Base," Barbara Price said over the headset. "Over."

Katz broke into a sprint as bullets from the terrorist vehicles sprayed the van. Engines roared as the drivers prepared to evade the impromptu blockade. The Israeli tapped the headset transmit button as he ducked behind the van and hunkered by the bumper. "Go, Stony Base. You have Phoenix One. Over."

"We're on-line here, Phoenix One. From our preliminary satellite scans, we've confirmed that this group belongs to Anvil of God. We've identified four people so far. Over."

"Affirmative," Katz responded. "It appears your Intel was on the money. Over."

Another man tried to break and run from one of the cars behind the lead truck. Calvin James or one of his sniping team brought the terrorist down. Katz could tell from the way the man fell, looking as if he'd been slapped down from above.

Katz shifted and raked a steady burst across the lead truck's front tires. The bullets turned the rubber to shreds that flapped from the steel rims. Control over the lumbering vehicle became instantly difficult.

Klieg lights mounted at strategic places flared into sudden bright life.

"Stony Base will be standing by," Price said.

Katz didn't acknowledge the transmission. The mission controller was well aware of the situation the team was in. Tied into a satellite thousands of miles out in space with video feed into the area, the Stony Man Farm support group knew exactly what was going on in the night-dark streets.

He thumbed the transmit button as the lead truck bore down on the van. "Gary."

"Just say when," the Canadian radioed back coolly.

"When."

"Get clear."

Katz pushed away from the van and raced for the fruit stand at the street side. Boarded up for the night with pull-down shutters, it promised little protection from the terrorist bullets. "Rafael," the Phoenix commander called out.

"I'm gone," Encizo radioed back.

Bullets licked at the concrete to Katz's left, drumming out a deadly tattoo that struck sparks from the steel drainage grate at the curb. Stone chips rained on the sidewalk as miniature potholes erupted in the smooth surface.

The harsh cracks of the M-21 Beretta and Galil sniping rifles overrode the drone of autofire. Tires screeched as other Mossad units pulled into position. Then the noise seemed to evaporate as a supernatural quiet enveloped the street.

Katz felt the concussion from the string of demolitions first, then heard the detonations roll over him like an ocean wave. He went to ground at once, aware of the vulnerable position he was in. Keeping his head covered protectively with his arms, he glanced back toward the battle on King David Street.

Armed with the foreknowledge of where the terrorist attack would take place, Gary Manning had mined the street, designing a mixture of munitions and mayhem to stun the terrorists and disable their vehicles. The mines had been placed so that the disruptive force would be aimed upward and not do any appreciable damage to the street. The mined area had been clearly marked by fluorescent tape placed at shoulder height on buildings to keep the friendlies out of harm's way, and to let Manning know no civilians were in danger.

The street mines worked in tandem, exactly as Manning had outlined. The car behind the lead truck had sat almost on top of two or more. When the explosives were touched off by the Canadian's remote-control detonator, the expanding force lifted the small Volkswagen and flipped it over on its side.

The terrorists started to leave their vehicles like rats deserting a sinking ship. White beams from the klieg lights played over them, providing eerie overtures as they lanced through the swirling dust raised from the street. Among the darting figures, the ruby ellipses of the snipers' laser sights streaked like bees. Men dropped as the heavy 7.62 mm slugs found flesh.

Katz pushed himself to his feet. He was satisfied with the action.

The lead truck had recovered to a degree, but flames clung to the rear section and were spreading across the tarp. Working frantically, the driver yanked the wheel and powered up again. Evidently damage from the explosives had caused him to kill the engine. The big motor rumbled as he guided it toward the rear of the van.

For a moment, Katz thought the van might hold. Then the greater weight of the truck tilted the balance. With a screeching metallic groan, the van slid out of the way, freeing the street for the truck's passage.

Katz tugged the yellow armband over his right biceps that identified him as one of the Mossad team, then sprinted after the truck. A statement was being issued in the streets of Jerusalem this night, and he wanted every *i* dotted and every *t* crossed.

As he drew abreast of the rolling truck, Katz was aware of a gunner leaning through the flaming tarp that covered the bed's metal skeleton. He prepared himself for the feel of a bullet thudding against his Kevlar vest, knowing he'd never be able to turn in time.

A harsh, flat crack ripped out over the street, descending from the heavens. Abruptly the gunner jerked forward and dropped from the fiery curtain of the canvas.

"Got you covered, Katz," James said over the headset.

Katz didn't respond. They were a unit, responsible for one another and the action set before them tonight. Personal thanks would wait until later.

The Phoenix Force commander launched himself at the truck. His prosthesis hooked over the lip of the door and held as his boots found the running board.

Hauling himself up, he levered the Calico over the door.

The driver's eyes grew large and frightened. A man seated in the back reached through the window opening onto the bed and pointed the revolver in his hand.

Katz made the adjustment, then squeezed the Calico's trigger. The rounds chopped into the gunner and flung him into the truckbed, slamming into the men there who'd been fighting the smoke and heat of their flaming coffin. Katz squeezed off a final round that took the driver in the temple. The man's body jerked behind the wheel, then slid limply to one side. His foot dropped heavily on the accelerator.

Out of control, the big truck jumped the curb and roared at a leather shop.

Katz released his hold on the door and dropped into a parachutist's tuck and roll. He came up on his feet as the truck slammed into the side of the two-story building. The Calico was at the ready as he jogged toward the truck.

The cobbled wall of the leather shop gave way before the powerful force of the assault. Rocks tumbled to the pavement. The brightly colored canopy over the shop's entrance shifted drunkenly, then came down like dropped sail, adding fuel to the fire clinging to the rear of the vehicle. Men scrambled from the truckbed of the truck, dressed in khaki uniforms and wearing keffiyehs.

Katz fired vicious figure eights that cut down the first wave, brass tumbling freely through the air. He stood his ground, under the partial cover provided by an olive tree standing tall in a planter built into the sidewalk.

"Yakov!" David McCarter's voice boomed. "Get your arse down! Now!"

Katz dropped to one knee and fired the last few rounds from the Calico. He reached for one of the 50-round drums and quickly slipped it into place with a reassuring click.

Out in the street, McCarter rolled to a halt in a battered Land Rover. A dead terrorist was draped facedown across the hood, obviously killed from a head-on impact. Bullets from the Anvil of God's guns ripped scars into the Land Rover's bodywork.

The lanky Briton scrambled from behind the wheel and moved up behind a .50-caliber Browning M-2 heavy machine gun mounted on top of the Land Rover. A hatch had been cut through the rooftop.

Katz fired again, taking down a man attempting to overrun his position.

Then the full-throated roar of the Browning opened up. The truck shivered from the impacts, and when the .50-caliber round found flesh-and-blood targets, they lifted them bodily from the ground.

In seconds it was over, leaving only bloody carnage behind.

Shouldering the Calico, Katz drew his side arm and advanced on the fallen terrorists. One of the men was seriously wounded but still tried to knife him. Katz shot the man through the head and walked on. Only corpses remained outside the truck.

Using his hook and shielding his face from the heat of the flames with his shoulder, Katz yanked the canvas open.

A wounded man crouched on the bench inside. He wore khaki trousers and a dark shirt. His features were shadowed by the keffiyeh, but his eyes gleamed in anger. In his hands was a block of white gray C-4 plastique already primed with a detonator.

"Drop your weapon," the man said calmly in Arabic, "or I'll blow us up."

Flames continued to devour the canvas overhead. Bits and pieces of charred fabric drifted to the truckbed.

"It makes no difference to me either way," the man promised. "Even when I am dead, the Wild Hunt continues."

Sizing up his options, knowing the man would react to any threatening movement on his part, Katz lowered his pistol. "David."

"I'm here, mate."

Katz never let his gaze leave the terrorist's, but out of the periphery of his vision, he saw McCarter standing to one side and behind him. The terrorist evidently hadn't registered the Briton's presence. "Can you take him?"

"Yes."

The terrorist struggled to his feet and started toward the rear of the truck. A broad bloodstain covered his shirt at his right side.

"Then get it done."

McCarter's Browning barked twice, and the terrorist's head jerked back. Both rounds had taken him in the face, somewhere between his eyes and mouth. He fell back, his body draping over a sheet of flame that had crept down from the canvas covering.

Knowing that the chunk of plastic explosive was only a small representation of the deadly cargo that had been aboard the truck, Katz vaulted into the vehicle. The heat seared his face and exposed skin, and the superheated air seemed almost too thin to breathe even when he dared to suck it into his lungs. He made his way forward, stepping over three corpses as he closed on the cab. Reaching through the tiny window, he found the small red fire extinguisher he'd seen earlier when standing on the running board.

He freed the extinguisher and pulled the safety pin. If the explosives went up, the amount of damage created by the well-timed raid would escalate dramatically. So far, he didn't think they'd lost any innocent lives.

"Katz!" McCarter bellowed over the headset. "Get the hell out of that bloody lorry, mate!"

Flame-retarding foam spewed out of the extinguisher nozzle, covering the crates. Katz wrapped his free arm over his nose and mouth to try to limit the amount of smoke he'd inhale. The metal tines of his hook were hot enough to burn his neck. Hot embers kissed his forehead. "Explosives," he croaked out.

"Oh bloody hell," the Briton responded. "Hold on."

Katz continued unleashing the pressurized contents of the extinguisher until it ran dry. A film of scum was left strung across most of the crates. There was no doubt that the fire was going to finish the job.

Without warning, a blast of cold, clear water surged through the opening and drove against the Phoenix Force commander. He staggered, caught off guard, and almost went down. His footing rapidly became treacherous, but the flames were beaten back almost instantly.

McCarter strode through the gaping canvas with his pistol in hand. A handkerchief was tied around his nose and mouth. "Out. Let's step lively, lad."

Katz went, his senses reeling from the smoke. He was covered with a sheen of perspiration.

"Stony Base to Phoenix One," Price called over the headset. "Over."

"Go, Stony Base. You have Phoenix One," Katz responded. He stood at the rear of the truck and watched a team of Israeli firemen approaching with their fire hose, their slickers already soaked. Beneath their helmets, their faces were grim and smeared.

"The last man who talked to you," the mission controller said.

"Yes."

"We recorded him on audio, but we didn't have a chance at video access."

Katz sucked in the cool air, then turned back to look for the man McCarter had shot. "Yes."

"Is he still alive?"

"No." The last of the flames flickered and died, but the firemen kept the deluge of water sluicing over the truck interior.

"He said something about the Wild Hunt?" Price persisted.

Katz took a moment to reflect. He saw Ranon Goldberg making his way through the cluster of uniforms ringing the area. Dressed in bulky protective armor and face shields, a bomb squad double-timed it to the truck. "Yes," he said.

"I need to see him," Price stated urgently. "As soon as you can arrange it."

Katz nodded at McCarter.

Dropping his Browning into shoulder leather, the Briton reached down for the dead terrorist and grabbed him by the shirt. He dragged him after Katz, not flinching at all when the body thudded against the hard pavement. He kept moving.

"Here," Katz instructed, waving uniformed cops and firemen back.

A crowd had gathered, and news media from domestic as well as international sources had become part of it. Videocamera floodlights played over the area, turning the surroundings into two-dimensional black-and-white cutouts at times.

Katz took a flashlight from his pocket, switched it on and shone the beam of light over the dead man's face. Tapping the headset's transmit button, he asked, "Can you see him now?"

"Yes." Price seemed preoccupied.

"Those words have some kind of meaning for you?" Katz asked.

"The term has been mentioned earlier tonight. In relation to a mission that Striker's involved with. I don't believe in coincidences."

The Israeli didn't, either. They happened, sure, but a trained warrior still questioned them if he wanted to remain among the quick.

McCarter lighted a cigarette and gazed down at the dead man. "Something's not right, mate." He let the smoke curl out of his nostrils.

James, an ex-SEAL, black and lanky, his upper lip dusted with a short mustache, knelt by the body. Trained in police science, he had a quick mind and was very resourceful. He was dressed in black jeans, joggers and a black sweatshirt. His combat harness held a variety of deadly weapons. A gold necklace glinted at his throat. His long fingers swept away the blood-soaked keffiyeh. "David's right. This cat ain't no Arab."

The face, except for the ruin caused by McCarter's bullets, was clean-shaved and angular. The hair was reddish blond, and his eyes, open in death, were blue.

"A ringer?" Manning asked.

"Or a pointman," Encizo replied.

"He handle English okay?" James asked, opening the man's mouth and peering inside.

"I don't know," Katz said. "He spoke Arabic with an accent."

"Well," James said, "the dental work's probably American. No gold, which the Europeans use a lot, and a couple of crowns that I can see, suggesting that he's probably been somewhere an insurance policy's been offered. That sounds like the States to me."

McCarter took a small stiletto from a sheath on his calf, then slit the man's sleeves to the shoulders with deft movements while James and Encizo went through his clothing. "Figure him as military too, lads," the Briton said. "Probably Special Forces at one time." He pulled back the sleeve on the left arm, revealing a black panther tattoo on the man's forearm. "Here's the clincher." He pulled the right sleeve up.

"A tattoo of a heart with *Mom* in it," Manning joked quietly.

The second tattoo was definitely military, possessing swords and a military slogan that had faded over the years.

Katz played the beam over the tattoo, squinting to make out the words. "Semper Fi."

"A jarhead," James said. "That makes him American."

Katz tapped the transmit button. "Stony Base, are you copying this?"

"Affirmative, Phoenix One. We're running his profile now."

"There's no ID." A small pile of change, extra pistol shells, a detonator, an ink pen and a compass were spread before James. "But there is this." He turned the compass over, revealing the beer bottle cap mounted there.

"Personalized," Encizo commented.

"That's a Vietnamese beer," McCarter volunteered. "It's not exported. Chances of him having that compass are slim."

"Something else," James said. He folded the man's left arm over so Katz could play the beam over it. Dark spots hovered just below the skin. The ex-SEAL tapped a forefinger against the inside of the elbow. "Needle marks. At one time this guy was a pretty heavy user. Been awhile, though."

"To make a change like that," Manning said, "guy must have been highly motivated."

James felt the man's chest, arms and legs. "Until tonight, he'd been in good shape. With a history like that, Stony Base, you might be able to ID this guy through NCIC."

"Only one of several possibilities at this point," Price answered.

An explosion sounded to the south, only a few blocks away. It was quickly followed by a string of others.

"That sounds like it's coming from the hotel," Encizo said, lifting his head and looking back along the street.

"That *is* the hotel, Phoenix," Price said. "Damn it! Somebody just hit the people we were supposed to be protecting. We're monitoring the security frequencies they're using at the King David Hotel."

Katz led the break toward the Land Rover McCarter had left parked at the curb.

Ranon Goldberg joined them, talking frantically over a radio handset. "We were set up," the Mossad chief said. "This—" he waved at the battleground laid around them "—was only a diversion."

Katz took the passenger seat while McCarter slid behind the wheel. The Land Rover started smoothly, then jerked into motion.

"If it was a diversion," the Phoenix Force commander said, "they paid a dear price for it."

McCarter weaved between the emergency-rescue vehicles with a radar sense, avoiding other bumpers by scant inches.

"You know these people, Yakov," Goldberg said as he clung to the outside running board. The rest of Phoenix Force was draped over the Land Rover. "They are passionate zealots."

Katz didn't point out the hyperbole. This was Israel, a land that had been constantly torn by war since its creation in 1948. In Israel, there were zealots and there were passionate zealots. It was the only way of dividing the peoples who dwelt there.

Two cars had been fire-bombed in front of the hotel and were wreathed in flames. The glass doors leading into the foyer had been shattered, and at least three bodies—two men and one woman—lay dead inside.

McCarter pulled the Land Rover to a halt, and the team scrambled from the vehicle. When Katz glanced up at the fires bleeding out of three of the upper stories, he knew they were too late.

Hotel security staff, beefed up by UN peacekeeping forces, met them at the front of the building with drawn weapons and shocked expressions.

Goldberg produced his ID and waved the guns away. He located the highest-ranking Israeli officer among the group and quickly got the story, bringing the man along as he and Katz went up in the elevator. The rest of Phoenix Force fanned out throughout the swank hotel.

It took bare moments to tell. Two groups had swept through the hotel while the Mossad group was ringing down the curtain on the Anvil of God terrorists. Four of the negotiators had been killed outright, another seven had been severely wounded. A second terrorist group, seemingly acting independently, had attacked the hotel itself, as well as the reporters in the bar who were filing late stories and talking shop. No one was sure how many people had been killed there. The terrorist groups had taken massive hits, as well, but it hadn't seemed to matter. The ones who had lived to fight another day had already faded the heat.

"Damn it," Katz swore softly. He looked at the destruction filling the area of the hotel where the people Phoenix force was supposed to be protecting should have been safe. There was no way Anvil of God would have acted in concert with another organization, even if they were both after Arafat's ass.

Yet there was no way to deny that that was what seemed to have happened. He hardened his emotions and went to sort through the carnage that had been left, hoping to find a handle on just what in hell was going on.

**10**

"I found some soup below deck." Dr. Elizabeth Parrish held out a steaming mug.

Bolan took it, maintaining a firm hand on the motor sailer's wheel. The warrior drank from the mug. In the hours he'd been tending to the steering, he'd numbed, dwindling down to an almost icy spark of soul. The soup warmed him.

"Coffee?" she asked, producing a weighted cup.

"Sure."

She stepped forward and took over the wheel. The wind whipped her hair. "I can handle this. Same course?"

"Yeah." Bolan let her take the wheel and stepped back. He'd had a lot of time to think while she'd been below deck. Without a secure line to Stony Man, he'd maintained radio silence for the most part. Whatever progress Price and Kurtzman might have made on the mystery of the Huntsman was unknown to him. They were working the history. He was more interested in making his next move. Someone had hired the Huntsman. Bolan wanted to turn up the money trail and follow it backward until he found out the other truths the Huntsman's name might be covering.

"I didn't find the radio transceiver on the body," Parrish said. She handled the wheel with confidence. "You're sure there is one?"

"As sure as I can be without being able to put my hands on it. And there's a very good chance that whoever I ran into back in Dover is still trailing us."

Parrish drew her long coat more tightly about her and gave the dark heavens an unconscious glance. "How much longer before we meet up with your friend?"

Bolan checked his watch. "Eighteen minutes."

She gave him a wan smile. "I like a man who's precise."

He studied the flat surface of the North Sea. It was much better suited for the pickup with Grimaldi than making the attempt in the choppy waters of the English Channel. Traffic there was also more risky. "What can you tell me about the woman?"

Parrish lapsed into a professional tone of voice and her eyes narrowed as she concentrated to review the mental file she'd obviously logged. "Early thirties. One hundred forty pounds, or thereabouts. Excellent physical condition, which masked the extra weight she'd carried. Her hair is dyed and is normally almost a mousy blond. Contact lenses altered the color of her eyes. Her dental work is good, probably American because her teeth are capped rather than merely being healthy. You Yanks have a tendency to go for the cosmetic."

Bolan checked the instruments and said nothing.

"She's been on drugs," Parrish continued. "There were needle marks on both ankles."

"Diabetic?"

She shook her head. "Not from my prelim. But it wasn't very long ago, and she had access to clean needles and didn't do her habit in the streets. The usual scarring from that kind of behavior wasn't present."

"But no fresh marks?"

"No."

"So she kicked the habit?"

"Or was put on some kind of drug rehab."

Bolan helped her make an adjustment on the wheel, following the marks he'd made on the compass. "How long ago?"

"Maybe a year. It's hard to say."

The warrior reviewed the discussion of the facts Price had assembled regarding the Huntsman and Annalee MacPherson. During that time, MacPherson had been working for magazines, and the Huntsman had been busy filling death contracts. It was hard to conceive that a junkie could do either. But there was no denying the needle marks.

"She suffered a rather grievous injury about four years ago," Parrish said. "Her left femur showed the signs and scarring from multiple fractures. Caused quite a mess from the looks of things. Whoever did the reconstruction did a hell of a job from what I can tell on the outside. Chances are, the doctor used steroids to initiate regrowth. That could account some for her physical build."

"But she'd have had to keep taking them."

"Right. That was a much smaller woman at one time. You can tell by the thickness of her wrists and ankles. Muscle growth like that doesn't come easily unless courted by discipline and drugs. Do you know what she did for a living?"

"Yes." Bolan looked at her, inviting her comments.

"At a guess, I'd say she was some kind of athlete."

"No."

"I'd have figured a long-distance runner or some type of endurance competitor. Maybe a swimmer."

"She was a reporter."

Parrish took that in and sipped her coffee. "Maybe a reporter with a physical-conditioning fetish."

Bolan turned that over in his mind. He'd noticed the way the woman was put together, and had logged the obvious effort she'd made toward keeping herself fit. He finished the rest of the soup and started on his coffee. In some regards, looking at the situation, Annalee MacPherson—or whatever her name ultimately turned out to be—had held the position of a specialty player and had only been called out for designated plays. Taking that into consideration, plus the fact that the Huntsman was reputedly a ghost anyway, and that Phoenix Force might have brushed up against a Huntsman in Jerusalem, the big warrior had to wonder how many other specialty players there were waiting on the bench.

"I'll know more, possibly, after I get the inside work done," Parrish said.

Bolan nodded.

The radio crackled and spit, then Jack Grimaldi's voice rattled through the speaker. "Striker, this is G-Force. Over."

"Go, G-Force, you have Striker."

"Bring me home, buddy, and let's get this show on the road. From the telesatellite link I have to base, it appears you've got aerial pursuit tracking you down. I'm closer, but they look like they might be faster."

"Affirmative, G-Force." Bolan activated the radio transponder he'd tuned to the frequency Grimaldi would be following to find them. He killed the engine, then went forward to drop anchor. Within minutes, the motor sailer came to a pitching halt and rolled on the gentle swells.

"We were followed," Parrish stated.

"Yes." Bolan loosened his jacket to allow quicker access to the weapons he carried. Most of them were short range, but the M-16/M-203 combination he had stored below deck gave him a longer reach. How effectual it would be remained to be seen.

He slid down the railings and approached the body. Parrish had redressed it after her inspection, preserving some of the woman's dignity after death. Moving quickly, the warrior furled the blanket back over the corpse. The doctor helped, both of them working against the pitch and yaw of the moored vessel. Bolan bound the blanket in place with ordnance tape.

"Is your friend going to reach us first?" Parrish asked.

"Could be a hell of a horse race," the warrior answered honestly as he shouldered the load. Balanced, he went forward, stopping only long enough to pick up the M-16/M-203.

On deck, he glanced toward the sky. To the west, a series of pinpricks of light drifted in their direction.

"Is that your friend?"

"No. He'll be coming from the south."

Fear briefly touched the doctor's features.

"It's possible the transmitter in the body doesn't broadcast all the time," Bolan said. "Burst transmission would downsize the unit we're looking for. It would also explain why we haven't been found until now. They've had to fly search patterns over the water until they picked us up."

"Well, they have."

Bolan glanced at the approaching lights. "Yeah."

Without warning, a new kind of distant thunder rumbled in the dark sky, and a fat-bodied shape dipped below the cloud cover. It took Bolan a moment to recognize the craft as a seaplane. He took a life raft from the on-deck storage compartment and triggered the self-inflating process. While it was shifting shapes, he tied a line to the raft and threw it overboard. In seconds it had completely expanded on the water. Using the flare gun tied to the railing, he fired three incendiary rounds onto the ocean surface. They skipped, then settled into position, lighting a triangular pattern almost seventy yards to a side.

The seaplane descended rapidly.

"Let's go," Bolan said. He eased the body into the bottom of the raft, then helped Parrish in.

"There'd better be a bloody big bonus in this," the doctor said. "Nobody said anything about sea rescue procedures or getting involved in gunfights."

Bolan grabbed the trolling motor from the storage compartment and clambered aboard the life raft. He attached the motor quickly. It fired to life on the first pull, and he set the raft's course for the area illuminated by the spluttering flares.

Like a diving swan, the seaplane settled onto the ocean, driving white spumes before the blunt body and pontoon-equipped wings. It came around, readying for immediate takeoff. The powerful engines rumbled over the relatively flat sea. The door popped open and Grimaldi stood waiting.

The raft bumped into the seaplane softly, and Bolan cut the engine.

Grimaldi leaned out and helped Parrish aboard. "Good to see you again, Sarge," the Stony Man pilot said to Bolan.

Bolan handed him the corpse. "Got to say the same, Jack."

The pilot took a last quick look at the approaching aircraft. "Helo."

"That's what I thought."

"It's going to be a near thing."

Bolan slammed the door while Grimaldi went forward. Parrish had already taken one of the rear seats in the small cabin and was tightening the safety belt. MacPherson's body lay on the floor. The warrior settled into the copilot's seat, the M-16/M-203 between his knees.

A strobe light lanced down from the body of the Bell helicopter skating low over the surface of the sea. It swept across the seaplane's rain-dappled windshields with temporarily blinding intensity.

Grimaldi adjusted the throttles, bringing the engines up to more speed. He watched through the windshield as the helicopter came about, hovering thirty yards above them and nearly a hundred yards out.

Abruptly a shooting star leaped from the side of the chopper and jetted toward the bobbing seaplane.

"Rocket launched," Bolan growled in warning.

"Right now, we're a sitting duck. But when I get into the air, I'm going to show them this duck's fangs."

The warhead slammed into the water less than twenty yards from their position. The sea threw up great waves that slapped into the seaplane, turning it violently.

"This is a Republic RC-3 Seabee," Grimaldi said as he started forward, gunning directly for the helicopter. "World War II vintage. Tough little bastard, and an excellent duck. She's cherry. I checked her out myself."

The engines screamed as they powered up. The Seabee roared forward, coming up out of the water as the propellers bit into the wind. The ride shifted from choppy to smooth. Two more warheads created traffic hazards before they were airborne.

Bolan fastened his safety belt. Grimaldi's skill with a stick in his hand was almost mystical.

The helo backed off, tracking them. Autofire opened up, knifing into the water, and a few stray rounds penetrated the Seabee's rear quarters.

"That helo can outrun us," Grimaldi said. "This plane was built more as a workhorse than as a thoroughbred. I take it they don't care if we're dead or alive?"

"No."

The Bell came at them with guns blazing, little lightnings flickering at the open cargo hatches.

"Hold on," Grimaldi said. The Seabee heeled over to the left, making a broad quarter circle that brought it up to the same altitude as the chopper, then came around until they were facing. The pilot flipped out a small electronic board that obviously wasn't original equipment. "In the war, these things were seldom armed. I figured on trouble tonight and arranged a little addition through a NATO center in France."

A miniature screen lighted up on the electronic board. Emerald cross hairs became visible, as an amber dot glowed near the center. When the amber dot was fully centered in the cross hairs, they turned crimson. Grimaldi punched a white button.

The helicopter had been approaching in a direct pattern, its guns firing infrequently with the angle all wrong.

Rocking back slightly, the Seabee shuddered for an instant, then righted itself. By that time a blazing inferno had enveloped the tail of the aircraft. The helo went down seconds later, smashing into the unforgiving sea and flying apart.

"Air-to-air missile," Grimaldi stated. "Got one in reserve if we needed it."

Bolan checked the dark sea, then used the infrared binoculars Grimaldi passed over. The pilot flew a tight circular pattern over the site. Separating the flotsam and jetsam was hard, eye-straining work.

"Got a live one down there," the warrior said. "Let's get him." He pointed out the survivor, floating belly-up in a life vest.

Grimaldi put the plane down easily, then powered toward the guy. He got within twenty feet.

Bolan opened the door and looked out at the man. The warrior held one of the Browning Hi-Powers, and he aimed it deliberately.

The man's frightened gaze locked with the Executioner's.

"I want to know who hired the Huntsman to kill the prime minister."

"I don't know," the man responded weakly. He stretched out a blood-covered hand. "You can't leave me out here like this."

"I can shoot you," the Executioner promised, "or let you freeze to death. Your choice."

"I don't know about the Huntsman. We were just hired to recover a body."

"Who hired you?"

The man appeared reticent.

Bolan fired a round that splatted into the water only a few feet from the man.

"Voight. A guy named Charley Voight. He's a connected guy. Maybe he'll know about this Huntsman guy."

Reaching back into the Seabee, Bolan took the line Grimaldi offered him, then tossed it to the man, who started making his way slowly to the seaplane.

"Do you have a secure line to Base?" Bolan asked.

The pilot nodded. "I take it I'm going to be filing a new flight plan."

"If I can get a lead on Charley Voight, bet on it."

CARL LYONS HUNKERED behind the big Chevy Suburban as it rolled toward the tobacconist's shop at the end of Baranof Avenue in Sitka, Alaska. He was dressed in black despite the rosy glow of dawn streaking the eastern skies. He was fully outfitted for the raid, carrying the Colt .45 Government Model in shoulder leather and the Colt .357 Python on his hip. Under his jacket, he wore a Kevlar vest and pouches carrying other pieces of quick-strike equipment.

The *India Moon* had been empty and riding high in the water when the Canadian Coast Guard had boarded the Russian freighter. A handful of eyewitnesses culled from the dockhands had given Able Team the name of Archangel Shipping, the transportation company who'd been waiting for the freighter and wasted no time in unloading her.

Price and Kurtzman had researched Archangel Shipping and found ties to a helicopter cargo service in Vancouver. A federal writ, granted by a Canadian judge, had given them access to the chopper service, but the guns hadn't been there, either. The trucking and chopper businesses weren't the only ones the Stony Man resources had turned up.

The same secret holding company that owned the two other businesses behind the scenes, also owned Three Saints Bay Tobacco Emporium in Sitka, and an adjacent apartment building. From what Price had been able to discover, the tobacconist shop had been one of the original trading posts on Kodiak Island in the 1780s. It had been purchased three years earlier, at the same time as the apartment building under another name, and a permit to build had been issued six months later.

The Three Saints Bay Tobacco Emporium was a single-story structure covered in wooden shingles that gave it a rustic appearance. Latticework windows were on both sides of the glass entrance and held advertising for different tobacco blends and pipes. Even a chimney pipe jutted from the angled roof and puffed gray smoke into the air. The only concession toward modern living, in addition to lighting, appeared to be the steel security bars behind the door and windows.

"Man," Schwarz said over the headset frequency, "take a look at that place, and you'd figure Daniel Boone would be in there at any time to bargain for a barrel of molasses."

Schwarz drove the Suburban and looked around as if searching for an unfamiliar address.

Golodkin and Blancanales were covering the back. A contingent of Alaska State Police recruited from Anchorage was backing the play. Sitka had less than ten thousand citizens, and the small domestic police force wouldn't have been up to the mission.

Lyons tapped the headset button. "Okay, look alive and let's put this operation down by the numbers."

"Mallet Leader, this is Javelin Three. I just spotted movement inside the building."

Lyons kept moving, but hitched up the Mossberg pump shotgun that was his lead weapon. The Javelin unit was a five-man team of snipers that had encircled the shop. "Stand ready, Javelin Three. Everything proceeds at my go. Just keep us apprised."

"Yes, sir."

The big ex-cop pressed forward. He was to take out the front door and make the way clear for the ground unit waiting in the wings.

"It's definite, sir," Javelin radioed. "They've noticed the truck."

"Keep on, Gadgets," Lyons said, glancing over the top of the Suburban's fender and peering through the series of windows until he could see the tobacco shop's door. He saw the pallid oval of someone's face come closer. Less than fifty feet remained between the truck and the front of the shop.

"He's got a gun," Javelin Three relayed with an edge in his voice.

Abruptly Lyons saw the man shove himself away from the door and head toward the back of the shop. The Able Team warrior pushed himself into motion, quickly leaving the Suburban as he pumped his legs. "Damn it! We're blown! Close it in! Pol, do you read?"

"We're on it," Blancanales replied.

Coming to a stop against the wall beside the door, Lyons reached for the small block of C-4 plastique he'd prepped for the door. As he reached to put it into place, the glass section of the front door exploded outward, accompanied by the sound of autofire.

Schwarz brought the mammoth Suburban to a halt to one side of the small, lined parking lot.

"Javelin Three requesting permission to fire."

"Take him," Lyons roared, then activated the detonator on the plastic explosive and ducked back. The sound of the sniper rifle cracked just before the C-4 exploded.

"He's down," Javelin Three announced.

Lyons whirled around the corner of the doorway and scanned the shop's interior. He saw the dead man lying between rows of tobacco products. The steel security bars were now a twisted maze. He had to kick the broken lock once to get the door to shudder open. When he entered, Schwarz was at his heels, holding an H&K MP-5.

Two men were at the back near a wall of ornate pipes and chess games. One of them popped up, holding a massive pistol.

Lifting the shotgun, Lyons fired. The double-aught buckshot cleared the gunner from the play immediately, bouncing his dead body from the wall and bringing down dozens of pipes. Lyons racked the slide and chambered another round as Schwarz squeezed off a burst of 9 mm rounds from the little machine pistol. Another dead man was stretched on the floor.

"There's a door at the back," Schwarz said. The first of the Alaska State Police were at the door, bulling their way through and taking up holding positions.

"I see," Lyons replied. "Pol?"

"Go."

"I got a back door."

"So do we."

Lyons took cover by the door a moment, then swung around and surveyed the interior. It was bare and little more than a closet space. "Mine's open."

"Not ours."

"These guys came from somewhere." The shop was still closed and wasn't supposed to open until ten o'clock. Lyons knew it was confirmation that they were close to their quarry.

"Wall at the back," Schwarz said. "It's not quite level."

Lyons looked and saw that the wall wasn't exactly flush. Upon closer inspection, he saw the soft glow of illumination behind it. He guessed at what had made the difference, then voiced it. "Pol, you guys cover the apartment house, too. They've dug in here. Got a regular rabbit's warren under this place."

"Roger," Blancanales responded.

Lyons moved on into the space, taking a thick-bladed combat knife from the sheath on his belt. He rammed it into the wall, crashing through the thin wood, then twisted and pulled. The section of wall came away, swinging easily on hinges.

A gunner crouched in the narrow corridor beyond. Firing the Mossberg one-handed, Lyons cleared the hallway, only then noticing the harsh sting of two rounds that had flattened against the bulletproof body armor. He took a deep breath to work the pain out of his system as he charged into the corridor.

The hallway ran almost twenty feet, lighted by dim bulbs, then turned right and became a series of steps. Lyons took them three at a time, almost falling down the incline.

Four men waited at the bottom of the stairs, obviously in a quandary as to what to do. All of them carried weapons.

There was no room for finesse. With a bloodcurdling yell that he emulated from a hundred Westerns he'd seen as a child, Lyons leaped at the enemy. He crashed into gunners, bowling them over. Recovering from the impact, he came up with the shotgun in both hands. He flailed out at the nearest man struggling to bring up a gun. The Mossberg's barrel caught the man in the chin and knocked him backward with the sound of splintering bone. He lashed out with a booted foot at another one, scoring on the man's forehead and rendering him unconscious. A third brought a submachine gun into play, firing blindly. A full-throated charge from the shotgun blew him away. The fourth man surrendered his weapon and lay facedown on the hardwood floor.

Turning, Lyons scanned the warehouse space beneath the tobacco shop and apartment building. Crates filled the center, and a table to the left held opened briefcases and scattered papers. A burst of autofire from behind one of the crates drove the Able Team warrior to cover beside the staircase. Schwarz was already in place and returning fire.

Lyons fished a smoke grenade from one of the pouches, armed it and flipped it toward the stacks of crates. The grenade went off with a loud pop and streamered smoke everywhere. He and Schwarz laid down covering fire while the Alaska State Police joined them.

Satisfied that they had the enemy on the run, Lyons moved more directly into the fray. He shoved shells into the shotgun, then touched off the first round, catching a gunner full in the chest as the man tried to open fire on one of the state policemen.

"Got the back door secured," Blancanales radioed. "They had a bolt hole in the apartment building. The manager was kind enough to show it to us after a little persuasion."

"Good," Lyons said. "Let's shut it down." Within minutes, the rest of the opposition were either dead or handcuffed. The state police led the live ones away and started loading them into waiting vans. In a town as small as Sitka, the media and casual onlookers weren't proving to be much of a problem.

Lyons took one of the wrecking bars they'd brought with them and started to open crates.

"Yes," Golodkin whispered as he peered inside. He took out one of the AK-47s and quickly inspected the serial number. "This is one of the series."

"I thought you said we were looking for Russian weaponry," Captain Ray Nicholson of the Alaska State Police said.

"We were," Lyons replied.

"Unless I miss my guess, this isn't Russian manufacture." He held up an M-16 A-2 and gestured toward the waist-high crate. "And there's plenty more where that came from."

"Something else, Ironman."

Lyons glanced over at Blancanales. His teammate stood beside another large crate and held what looked like a fistful of hundred-dollar bills. "What the hell is that?"

"Certainly looks like a cash crop to me," Schwarz volunteered.

Lyons joined them and found himself staring down into a crate of hundred-dollar bills.

Blancanales backed off from the box and gazed at it speculatively. "Sure looks like a ton of money to me."

"Geez," Lyons said as he ran a hand through the cash.

"It's counterfeit," Schwarz said. "Got a lot of different serial numbers here, but they are repeated." He held the bill up against the light and popped it between his hands. "Good paper, though."

American military weapons and counterfeit money hadn't been on Lyons's agenda. He couldn't wait to hear what Brognola and Price made of it.

**11**

The sign read Dwight Albertson's Alligator Farm. It was obviously hand-lettered across the crooked planks that had been nailed together to make the sign. It stood crookedly beside the worn red dirt trail leading to the homestead deep in the Dade County Everglades. Deep basso grunting filled the morning air, already pungent with the prevalent aroma of the marshy area.

"What's that?" Hal Brognola asked.

Behind the steering wheel of the Ford Bronco, Miami-based Treasury agent Michael Ferris smiled. "That's male gators in full rutting fever." His blond hair was flipped back up on his head in a fifties greaser style that didn't fit the three-piece suit.

"Terrific." Brognola reached in his pocket and got two antacid tablets. He chewed with deliberation.

Harry Wu, the field agent sent over by Hong Kong, leaned forward from the back seat, a smile splitting his round face. He wore black-rimmed glasses and short-cropped black hair. "Ah, the imagery that brings to mind. It would really spark up those Izod shirts, wouldn't it?"

Brognola didn't respond. So far, being nominated as leader of the international agency investigating the counterfeiting ring had been anything but a stone blast. There'd been more primping and posturing egos at the Miami hotel where they'd been checked into than at the White House on January 20 after a presidential election year.

"You got to watch these crackers down here," Ferris said. "With most of them, their families have been involved in illegal activities for so long, they shoot out of habit anybody who looks like they're from the government."

"Now there's a comforting thought," Brognola said. Deeper in the Everglades, a team composed of Dade County deputies and the international task force were closing in on the alligator farm as well, in a carefully designed pincer movement. Personally the big Fed felt like it made as much sense as hunting mice with hand grenades. He reached for the walkie-talkie he was carrying.

Ferris pulled to a stop in front of a leaning, single-story structure. Here and there split-rail pens stood up like broken and decayed teeth in the yard. Mud covered the ground like a lawn, and long two-by-twelves made low bridges across the swampy depths.

"Can you say anomaly?" Ferris asked, pointing at the satellite dish almost out of sight behind the house. "I guess it keeps down the boredom level when the gators' libidos aren't at full peak."

Brognola opened the door and got out, automatically reaching for his shield case. He scanned the front of the house and, when he felt the short hairs on the back of his neck rise, knew he was being watched.

The front door opened and a long, skinny man who went shirtless under his overalls came out, one hand under his bib scratching his narrow chest. "Help y'all?"

"Are you Dwight Albertson?" Brognola asked, taking out the warrant from his jacket pocket.

Albertson and his clan had turned up in Dade County Sheriff's files as suspected traffickers. Kurtzman had put a lock on the link by sifting through the disbursement points for the counterfeit cash. On three different occasions, relatives of Albertson had been involved. Brognola didn't fault the regular police agencies for not discovering the links, because they didn't have the sheer spectrum of resources open to the Stony Man computers.

"Yes." Albertson's eyes narrowed in quick suspicion. "Figured you fellers were just lost." He took a step back toward the house.

"Hardly." Brognola offered the papers. "Got a writ here that entitles me to search the premises."

"I guess I ought to talk to my lawyers about that."

The big Fed's voice hardened. "After."

"Don't see how you can come on my property like this," Albertson said plaintively. "I ain't done nothing wrong."

"If you haven't, then you haven't got anything to worry about."

Without warning, a window sash moved at Albertson's side. "Get the hell out of there, Pa," a young man's voice yelled. A rifle barrel poked out of the window, shredding the screen.

Brognola unlimbered the .357 he carried in a paddle holster on his hip and dodged behind the door for cover. Ferris peeled off to the left, cutting in close to the house. Wu and Napier, the French representative, went to ground behind an overgrown flower bed set off by railroad ties.

Albertson disappeared into the house just as an assault rifle cut loose.

Ducking behind the Bronco's door, Brognola sidled around and took deliberate aim at the window where the rifleman stood. He squeezed off three rounds, joined seconds later by Napier and Wu. Ferris had made the side of the house and was waiting to make his move.

"What the hell's going on?" a man's whiskey-rough voice blasted over the walkie-talkies.

Brognola recognized the speaker as George Cosgrove, the other Treasury agent based in Miami. The man was ex-military and not very accepting of outside intervention in agency affairs. He hadn't liked Brognola from the beginning.

Ferris quickly responded to his partner's question. More guns joined the first, drilling holes in the Bronco's bodywork and glass.

"Cover me," Brognola instructed the Hong Kong and French agents, who nodded.

He went into motion with both hands on the .357, sprinting for the front door. Bullets dug at the mud under his feet. When he heard the sudden chorus of autofire kick in, he thought he'd made a mistake and was dead on his feet. Then he realized the new barrage was coming from the woods behind the house.

Frenzied snatches of conversations flickered across the walkie-talkie frequency. In seconds he knew the teams coming in from behind the house had evidently flushed a delivery team and were involved in a full-scale firefight.

Ferris appeared at the other side of the door, his face grim. "Ready for the door?"

Feeling the old tension settling into his stomach, Brognola nodded. "I got high, and I'm right on your heels."

"Let's do it." Ferris swung around the door and barreled inside.

Brognola was right behind him. The furniture in the small living room was fairly new but badly treated, too much for the size of the room and centered around a large-screen television that blocked a pair of windows.

Three men were in the room at the windows, all of them with Albertson's thin, rangy build. A young man with straw-colored hair wheeled about and brought a .30-30 with him.

Brognola shot the gunner twice in the chest, bouncing him off a wall and bringing down a shelf covered with family cameos and whatnots. Ferris put down another one. Firing his final round, the big Fed put a bullet through the third man's shoulder, putting him out of the action.

"The hallway," Ferris shouted, heading for the narrow opening.

Wu and Napier crowded in through the front door and covered the surviving gunman.

Brognola shook out the empty brass and put in six more shells with a speed-loader from his jacket pocket. He trailed Ferris and found the younger Treasury agent peering down an opening in the floor of the main bedroom. An old, faded woman dressed in jeans and a pale pink blouse sat on the rumpled bed and hugged herself fiercely, not looking at either of them. Her hair was pulled back in a severe bun.

"Bolt hole," Ferris said. An unlighted coal-burning lantern hung from a peg in the earthen wall. The opening had been hidden by a rug, and the door looked as if it had been cut from the flooring. He shone a penlight into the depths. A narrow stream of muddy water twisted across the bottom of the tunnel. "Shallow. Maybe ten feet deep, and the passageway can't be over four feet high." He tested the wooden ladder hammered into the ground below and tied into the floor underpinning.

"Enough to do the job," Brognola said. "Which way does it go?"

"South." Ferris moved the penlight back and forth, obviously uneasy about going down into the hole.

Brognola figured the run in his head, coming up with the barn south of the house as the probable destination. He spoke his thoughts.

"Can't tell for sure from up here," Ferris said. "Damn it." He levered himself into the hole.

"You keep your eyes open down there, junior." Brognola turned and ran for the door, rattling information over the walkie-talkie quickly. The sheriff had arranged for two marked units to be on the main road away from the turnoff as reserves. Brognola called them in as he clambered behind the wheel of the Bronco. Ferris had left the keys in the ignition. The 4WD fired up on the first try.

Engaging the transmission and slipping it down into four-wheel drive, Brognola headed toward the barn. He kept an ear out for the conversations coming in over the walkie-talkie. The second team of agents had the delivery people in hand now, but there was no contraband, only empty airboats, suggesting that they'd already made their delivery.

Fifty yards out from the barn, Brognola watched the structure's double doors explode outward as a fully dressed Dodge Ram barreled through them. Whip antennas equipped with bobcat tails were bent like rainbows over the truckbed. At least five men were in the double cab.

Alligator pens lined both sides of the narrow trail leading away from the barn toward Brognola. The big Fed held his course even though bullets chopped into the windshield.

Panicked, the Dodge Ram's driver tried to slam on the brakes to lose speed and go around the Bronco. Brognola pulled the wheel over viciously, hitting the truck squarely in the side and flipping it over an embankment beside one of the alligator pens.

Jarred from the impact, the Justice man was a little slow in getting out of the 4WD. His polished shoes sank in the loose mud as he ran toward the pen. The excited grunts of the reptiles echoed inside the depression.

The truck had landed on its side up against the alligator pen rails. Dwight Albertson climbed out of the driver's-side window. Two other men were already standing outside the truck, pistols in their fists.

"Drop the guns!" Brognola ordered as he came up over the embankment.

Both men spun to face him. One leveled his side arm, aiming at Brognola. The big Fed pulled the trigger twice, working the .357's double action and riding out the recoil.

The gunner fell with a short scream, tumbling over the low railing to land inside the alligator pen. Brognola heard the sound of movement almost immediately, heavy flesh being dragged across the slick, gripping mud. There was a snap of jaws.

"God Almighty!" Albertson croaked, his face going pale as he watched the violence in the alligator pen.

"Your choice," Brognola told the other gunman.

After a brief hesitation, punctuated by occasional meaty smacks of chewing, the man threw his pistol into the mud and held up his hands.

"Against the railing," Brognola directed, using the .357 to point. The man complied. "Now down, against the poles." When the man got down, the big Fed snapped a pair of handcuffs on the man and threaded them through the rails. The sight on the inside of the alligator pen chilled him.

An alligator, at least a dozen feet long, was savaging the corpse that had dropped into the pen, working on the shoulder and neck. The body was almost decapitated. Two other reptiles were nearly submerged in the mud and advancing on the first cautiously. In retaliation, the big alligator yanked its head around and opened its mouth wide in warning, exposing bloody fangs and a pinkish-white tongue. The other two alligators retreated reluctantly.

"You can't let him do that to Willie," Albertson said. "It ain't right."

"He's dead," Brognola replied harshly, trying to ignore the nausea that seethed inside him. A quick glimpse inside the overturned pickup showed him that one of the other men was dead, as well. The fifth one was unconscious. Two M-16s lay spilled across the seats.

Footsteps sounded to Brognola's right, and he swung the pistol around to cover whoever was approaching.

Ferris came over the rise, mud-splattered and his face red from exertion. When he saw that Brognola apparently had everything under control, he leaned forward with his hands on his knees. "Barn's full of weapons," he gasped. "American military rifles, pistols and other small arms."

"The counterfeit?" Brognola asked.

"It's there."

Brognola turned to Albertson. "Who's supplying you?"

Albertson attempted to straighten his spine and face the bigger man. "Don't have to talk to you. I got lawyers. I got rights."

Anger welled up in Brognola when he remembered how many people could be hurt by the counterfeit currency. When economies took a hit, it was the little people who hurt most. Albertson and his brood had shown no compunction about taking lives themselves.

Brognola stepped forward, invading the older man's space, and wrapped the fingers of his big hand around Albertson's neck. Bulling forward, he forced the man up to the split-rail fence, then bent him sideways over it.

The two alligators approached eagerly, tails whipping to balance their heavy bodies as they worked their short legs. Their mouths opened in anticipation.

"They're going to bite me!" Albertson shrilled.

Not far away, the third alligator was feeding vociferously on the corpse.

"Give me a name," Brognola demanded. Albertson squirmed in his grasp, gripping his forearm with both hands and kicking against the fence in an attempt to get away.

"You're crazy! They'll bite your arm off clean up to the elbow!"

The alligators were less than two feet away and closing. The mud sucked at them audibly as they coasted through it.

"A name," Brognola repeated.

The nearer alligator threw itself forward, its beady eyes burning black.

"Harrison Cordwainer," Albertson shouted. "Jesus God, get me away from that thing!"

The alligator's jaws snapped closed, narrowly missing the man's head.

"Tell me about the guns," Brognola insisted.

"Part of a new deal," Albertson said, his eyes rolling bloodshot white. "I was holding them for one of those gangs out of Atlanta, Georgia. God, I'll talk. Just get me out of here."

Hauling the man out of the pen, Brognola shoved him at the ground, then turned and emptied his gun into the feeding alligator's head. Scarlet twisted into the river of mud. Reloading, he quickly killed the other two before they could turn on the corpse.

"You just killed three specimens of an endangered species."

Brognola shook the brass out of the .357 and reloaded, turning to find George Cosgrove standing beside Ferris. A half-dozen deputies and three of the foreign policemen stood behind him. "Sue me."

Cosgrove took an unfiltered cigarette from behind his ear, then flicked a kitchen match with his thumb and lighted it. "If I'd been running this show, things would have gone a lot smoother."

"You had your shot at it," Brognola said. "Now it's my ball and my bat, and I make the rules. If you don't like it, take a hike."

Color flared in Cosgrove's face. The whole team had sensed the enmity between the Washington Fed and the Miami-based agent from the start. They were all team players, and an undercurrent of tension like that couldn't be ignored.

Ferris smiled and clapped his partner on the shoulder. "Hey, lighten up. The good guys won this one, and that's all that matters. And this guy's got an interrogation technique that's got to be seen to be believed."

Cosgrove flipped his cigarette into the mud. It hissed and sizzled out as he turned and walked away.

Brognola was aware the situation hadn't been alleviated but knew he'd deal with it if he had to. Holstering his weapon, he turned to the assembled teams and began making assignments. A lot of information about the trafficking network was there to be had if they worked at it. He was anxious to see where the trail would take them.

"Mr. Thone?"

Thone took the cellular phone from the caddie and retreated from the foursome he'd been golfing with. Colonel Randall Schat, retired, was addressing the ball on the fourth tee while two of his friends looked on. Thone was familiar with the course; he was a member. The fourth hole was a rough dogleg with plenty of sand and water traps, a hard par five. "Hayden Thone."

The early-morning sun blazed down over the golf course, igniting the greensward and the white golf carts trundling across it.

"Your man in gay Paree," De Moray said with cheerful brightness.

"Yes?"

Schat swung well and the ball carried a good two hundred yards out, arcing high before dropping back to earth.

"Sadly, Jacques Villon, munitions king, died in his sleep last night. Apparently his water bed developed a bad leak that dripped down into the surge protector under the edge of the bed. He was electrocuted. Somewhat painfully, I might add."

"Good," Thone said. "I need you in England as soon as you can get there."

"Problems?"

"I have need of your talents again, my friend. It appears there's someone there whom you might even find challenging. He's become something of a thorn in my side, and I've got more than enough trouble already." Thone knew that was an understatement. He'd taken considerable losses in both Alaska and Miami, without adding the rat's nest that could be uncovered from the Huntsman assassination attempt against the English prime minister.

"When?"

"As soon as you can get there. I'll be forwarding specifics." Thone broke the connection and handed the cellular phone back to the caddie, tipping the boy a five-dollar bill. He took his wooden driver and a ball and tee. Planting the tee in the ground, he sat the ball on top of it and concentrated, letting his breath out naturally.

"Business call?" Schat asked. He was in his late fifties, with a full head of silver hair and muddy drinker's eyes that emphasized the broken capillaries in his thin nose.

Thone addressed the ball and took a practice swing. "Yes."

"Good or bad?"

"Good."

"That's nice," Schat said. "I figured when you decided you wanted to go on this little golf game, things might be going kind of rough for you. The last time we talked, you told me my price was too high."

"It still is." Thone glanced up at the retired military man. "Still, I like to think that you're a reasonable man."

"I heard about the weapons being seized in Canada and Alaska, and a few minutes ago I learned that another cache of American military weapons was uncovered in Dade County, Florida."

Thone pulled the club back and swung hard. The ball sped fast, hard and true, landing a good seventy yards farther than Schat's.

"Figured those might belong to you," Schat said. "If so, I thought you might be in a pickle. There's a shipment going out soon from Rome, but you're going to have to move fast if you're going to get it."

"American weapons?" Thone asked. The other two men were Schat's toadies, bought and paid for.

"Yes."

Thone slid his club into his bag and walked with the man to the golf cart. "The price?"

"Is more." Schat shrugged sorrowfully. "It's a seller's market now, and the risk has gotten greater. You could be found out. You're definitely running a risk of more exposure."

"I can handle things."

Schat got behind the wheel while the other men climbed aboard another cart. "Sure you can." He slapped Thone on the knee. "Never doubted that for a minute. Now let's talk about money." He named a figure.

"That's twenty percent higher than the last time we talked," Thone protested, holding on to the edge of the cart as it rattled down the incline.

"Yep. That's the only deal on the table, son. I'm risking my pension here, as well. Put in a lot of years for that, serving this country. Lot of bullshit under the bridge."

Thone knew he had no choice. And somehow Schat had sensed that. Quietly he agreed. A broker with nothing to broker was quickly out of business. He knew he was going to have to step up the timetable on the Huntsman operation to try to balance things out.

Schat climbed out of the cart and hit his ball, then drove on to Thone's.

Thone addressed the ball, knowing he would have to hook it left to clear the water trap over the trees in front of him.

"One other thing," Schat called out. "I want to win this game. For a change. Something to remember."

Resisting the anger that stirred inside him, Thone pulled the club back and swung. Flying straight and true, the ball dropped into the center of the water trap with a loud plop.

"Too bad," Schat clucked enthusiastically.

Returning to his seat in the cart, Thone said, "Now tell me about Rome."

"BLOODY HELL," David McCarter said as he scrambled across the dust-strewed hills and closed on the target area.

"Not bloody hell," Gary Manning chided from nearby, "Bloody Wind."

"Right, mate." McCarter gained the top of the rise and peered over the desert landscape. Israel was a country drowning in sand. Every fertile area reclaimed from the sea and from the desert was an exercise in hard work and clever engineering.

Before him on the plateau, an old stone fort that had been abandoned years earlier stood like a monument. The area was east of Jerusalem, near the Jordanian border and north of the Dead Sea. The fort had supposedly been empty for years. The ex-SAS warrior now knew that wasn't the case.

A small Cessna cargo plane sat idling in front of the building as men in robes hurried to ferry crates from the fort and into the belly of the plane.

"Think they figure we found out about them?" McCarter asked.

"I believe someone mentioned it might be a possibility after last night," Manning replied. Like McCarter, he was dressed in desert camous.

Taking a pair of field glasses from his backpack, McCarter lay on his belly and surveyed the scene. He was dressed for the strike Katzenelenbogen had outlined. The Browning Hi-Power was in shoulder leather, with an identical pistol at his hip. For a lead weapon, he carried a Galil Model 332, chambered in the heavier 7.62 mm round. There were more of the terrorists on hand than he'd expected. With a few more sweeps of the binoculars, he located the motor pool of jeeps and Land Rovers at the side of the fort.

Until that morning, not much had been known of the Bloody Wind terrorist faction. Like Anvil of God, Bloody Wind thought the Palestinians got a raw deal from Israel. They'd maintained a surprisingly quiet profile so far, though. If it hadn't been for the weapons many of the Anvil of God terrorists and the second group had carried the previous night, it wouldn't have been so critical to find out about them.

A number of the weapons that had been used had been of Russian manufacture, which wasn't surprising in itself. But many of them were also of sequential serial numbers, suggesting that the two groups had gotten their guns from the same supplier. The Mossad interrogators had been unrelenting and had broken men in both organizations. To a man, they'd admitted that the weapons had been supplied by the Bloody Wind.

McCarter and the other men of Phoenix Force had recognized the significance at once. Although the splinter groups had denied working together, had in fact all purported to have gathered intelligence themselves and chosen to attack last night, the arms tied them as a single unit.

"Phoenix One to Phoenix Two. Over."

"Go," McCarter responded, shifting the ear-throat headset around so he could speak. Katz's voice carried clearly.

"Are you in position?"

"Affirmative."

"You and Phoenix Three will take out the plane on my signal."

"Acknowledged, mate." McCarter surveyed the hills on the other side of the fort. The plan was simplicity: when he and Manning took out the plane, all eyes would be on them and would allow Katz and his group to roll up from behind in the helicopters and jeeps they'd requisitioned for the fast strike.

Manning shifted in the loose sand and brought out the Tank Breaker they'd packed for the assault. There were two extra missiles for optional targets. The big Canadian stood up on his knees behind a large boulder and shouldered the antitank weapon.

McCarter loaded it with efficiency, then tapped Manning on the back of the head to let him know it was ready. He fisted another rocket and waited.

"Phoenix Two," Katz called.

"Ready."

"Do it."

"Right, mate."

Manning squeezed the trigger, rocking back with the recoil.

Operating off IR targeting systems, the warhead arced up, then came smashing down on the Cessna's cabin. The explosion was blinding. Bits of the aircraft became deadly shrapnel that chewed into the Bloody Wind terrorists.

McCarter reloaded and tapped Manning. The Canadian, seeing that the plane was finished, moved on to the fort. The warhead flew true and smashed into the side of the building, creating a gaping hole that leaked dust and mortar. More of the terrorists went down from the concussion. Abruptly the Cessna jerked in its death throes as the munitions aboard touched off in a deadly series of explosions.

The terrorists wasted no time in returning fire. The section of the plateau where McCarter and Manning had taken up positions was quickly peppered with small-arms fire. They took cover.

McCarter tapped the transmit button on the headset. "Phoenix One, if you blokes are ready for the cavalry charge, it would be bloody convenient for us. These blokes are intent on turning us into colanders."

"On our way," Katz answered.

"I got one rocket left," Manning said, sitting with his back to the boulder.

McCarter hunkered beside his teammate. "You feel lucky?"

"As a three-balled tomcat."

McCarter scrambled over to his side of the boulder and peered around the edge. The terrorists were surging toward their position, laying down covering fire as they advanced in waves. A Land Rover with a mounted machine gun was racing up to the front of the ragged line. The Briton fisted the Galil. "You're going to have to make it a good one, mate. We have a vehicle bearing down on us that's going to blow Katz's rescue operation all to blazes if you don't.''

"Where?"

"One o'clock. Two hundred yards out and closing like a proper bastard."

"I'm on it."

McCarter leaned out and returned fire. The Galil rattled off 3-round bursts with precision, then he heard the whoosh of the Tank Breaker firing the remaining round.

The Land Rover jumped a sand dune as the four-wheel drive propelled it forward. Then the front end became a twisted mass of fiery wreckage as the vehicle flipped backward, taking out more of the terrorists in the process.

In the background, beyond the curving line of the horizon, a dust cloud rose up. Through it, with effort, McCarter could make out jeeps and military transport trucks. A heartbeat later, four helicopters streaked into view above the ground vehicles.

The terrorists became disoriented, unable to decide whether to pursue their first aggressors or flee from the approaching small army.

Manning took up his M-16/M-203 combo and pumped 40 mm warheads among the ground troops within range.

Firing deliberately, using the scope on the heavy Galil, McCarter wreaked vengeance against the Palestinian terrorist group. A number of good people had died in the previous night's raid without a chance to defend themselves, and even if the Bloody Wind hadn't been directly responsible for those assassinations, they'd supplied a number of the weapons. He changed magazines and carried on the attack until the terrorists began throwing down their weapons. It was almost disappointing how quickly they'd seen how foolish resistance was.

A jeep roared up the incline as McCarter lighted up a cigarette. Calvin James was behind the wheel, dusty and drenched with perspiration.

"Want a ride, guys?" the ex-SEAL asked.

McCarter and Manning clambered aboard. "Where's Rafe and Katz?" the Briton asked.

"Coordinating the search-and-seizure stuff. Barb called us to let us know she had an interest in the weapons we turned up."

"How so?"

James guided the jeep back toward the remains of the fort. "Seems the serial numbers tie up with something Able's been working on in Alaska."

"These blokes do get around, don't they?" McCarter asked.

The radio frequency in the headsets flared to life without warning, creating a painful squelch. All three men jerked in response. Then a deep, rich voice filled the airwaves.

"You people are fools," it said. "No one can stop the Huntsman. The Wild Hunt *will* continue."

James pulled the jeep to a halt in front of the fort. Katz stood in the doorway. "What was that about?"

"Apparently they were able to get a message off," the Phoenix Force leader said. "We found radio equipment inside."

"Who the hell's the Huntsman?" McCarter asked.

Katz waved at one of the terrorists handcuffed and on his knees by the door. "Apparently he's the man who's been running the Bloody Wind. He's the person responsible for getting them the guns."

Barbara Price's voice cut in over the headset. Stony Man Farm had been monitoring the raid via telesatellite. "He's more than that," the mission controller said. "We need to talk. Some place private, Yakov."

"Yes," the Israeli replied. "I think so, too."

**12**

Mack Bolan threaded his way through the traffic jam that lingered on the Strand. Crossing over the Thames River by way of Blackfriars Bridge had been no problem. But the midday traffic was too confining. In its day, that section of London had been designed more for hansom cabs and walkers.

Giving up, he turned the rental car east on Queen Victoria Street and made his way to Saint Paul's Cathedral and dumped the vehicle. He got out and walked, his destination a little over a mile away west on Fleet Street.

The pedestrian traffic was thick, as well, but flowed along much faster than the vehicular transportation. A red double-decker bus roared by with chronic belching from the exhaust.

The warrior was dressed in casual business attire, wearing a tan poplin jacket over brown slacks and a white shirt with a chocolate tie. He blended in with the working-class crowd around him. Until the late 1980s, Fleet Street had been the center of English journalism. The bars where the news reporters had gathered were still in business, as were the restaurants and various other businesses that had flourished with the newspaper trade.

He carried a Browning Hi-Power in shoulder leather under his left arm, and a handful of extra clips were in his jacket pockets. A Gerber Mark II combat knife was sheathed on his left calf.

Grimaldi was sitting tight at Heathrow Airport, under a curtain of diplomatic immunity provided through Stony Man Farm resources. After she'd finished the autopsy, Parrish had quietly faded back into her routine life.

The autopsy itself hadn't yet yielded any other useful information. But the doctor did recover the transmitter. Kurtzman had been able to triangulate the signal's chief receiver during one of the transmission bursts. The address had been the same one that Price had turned up for Charley Voight.

According to the mission controller's Intel, Voight had once been a member of the British intelligence community, had spent some time in MI-6 before being released during a scandal that had included plenty of dirt but nothing substantial enough to land the man in jail. By all accounts, Voight was a dangerous man with plenty of resources at his command.

And the Executioner was planning on bearding the man in his lair.

He walked briskly, covering the distance in long strides.

The building where Voight had his offices was in an art deco monstrosity of black glass and chrome that had once housed one of the larger daily papers. On the surface, Voight was now a foreign-employment representative, placing laborers and professionals in other countries as well as bringing them into Great Britain. His income-tax statements reflected that he made a good living at it. It was also, Bolan knew, a good cover for someone who needed to move people around who were supposed to remain invisible.

Bolan acknowledged the doorman with a nod and passed through, ignoring the building map in the middle of the foyer. Price had already faxed him enough information that he knew the layout of the building.

He avoided the elevators and took the stairs. At the third-floor landing, the warrior turned into the main corridor and eventually found a small bronze door that advertised Voight International Employment Services in gilt letters.

Bolan tried the door, and it opened.

A receptionist sat at the other end of a large waiting room behind a desk with an inlaid wood surface. She was small and petite, and very polite. "May I help you?"

"I'm here to see Mr. Voight." Bolan came to a halt at the desk and surveyed the room. Expensive prints of foreign landscapes covered the walls, and the potted plants looked well cared for.

"Of course." The receptionist leaned forward and consulted her appointment book. "You're American?"

"Yes."

She looked up at him and smiled. "I can tell. No offense. It's just a game I play with myself. I get to hear so many accents every day."

Bolan nodded understandingly.

"What is your name?"

"I don't have an appointment."

A flustered look filled the woman's face. "I'm sorry. Mr. Voight probably won't be able to see you today, then. He's been very busy of late."

"If you let him know, I'm sure he'll see me. I'm an old friend."

"No, I really can't do that. Mr. Voight's in an important meeting and left me strict orders that he's not supposed to be disturbed."

"That's all I needed to know," Bolan said. He slipped the Browning out of shoulder leather and walked toward the door behind the desk. "Scram before you get hurt."

With a gasp, the woman stood and fled her desk.

Bolan stepped through the door into a maze of modular offices made of movable walls and glass. He followed the blueprints Price had included in the faxes, turning right.

Although the building itself didn't have a security guard during the day, the woman would notify the London police at her earliest convenience. The warrior knew he was already racing the numbers on the play.

A few of the modular offices were occupied. He used the pistol and his voice of command to clear them, sending them all out through the main entrance.

Just as the entrance to the main conference room came into view, the warrior spotted a man in a dark suit who made a grab at a weapon holstered under his jacket. The guy didn't hesitate about firing as Bolan dodged for cover.

Bullets drilled through the glass front of the office the Executioner had ducked into and dropped jagged shards onto the carpet. The hollow booms of the big handgun sounded like thunder in the narrow spaces.

Bolan whirled around the door frame with the Browning level before him, the butt resting in his empty palm. He kept both eyes open and centered on the gunner. Squeezing quickly, he fired four rounds, tracking up from the man's belt buckle to his eyes. Bloody patterns splattered onto the antique-white wall of the conference room.

On the move immediately, the Executioner dipped a hand into his jacket pocket for a fresh clip, then approached the conference-room door.

A broad man with a large-caliber revolver opened the door.

The Executioner shot the man five times, the 9 mm rounds driving the corpse back into the room before the nervous system finally collapsed and died. Bolan stepped into the room.

It was almost thirty feet long and twenty feet wide. Potted trees stood in two of the corners of the room opposite each other, their emerald green leaves standing out against the blue gray of the unadorned walls on three sides. The fourth wall that overlooked the street was a floor-to-ceiling black glass slate. A long table occupied the center of the room, surrounded by leather chairs the color of the walls. Four men were in the room, pushing themselves up from the table. A door stood open in the rear wall.

Charley Voight stood at the head of the table in front of several typed forms and a yellow legal pad. He was in his late fifties, thirty pounds too heavy in spite of being over six feet in height, and had a florid face. His gaze was locked on to the dead man lying at the foot of the table.

The three men with him were all younger and didn't hesitate in reaching for the guns snugged in various holsters under their jackets.

The Executioner swept from left to right, placing two shots each in the first two men. After the fourth shot, the Browning blew back empty.

The first two men spun, slammed by the 9 mm rounds and knocked off balance. But the third man was left intact. He brought up the Intratec 9 machine pistol in both hands and squeezed the trigger.

Already in motion, Bolan felt the rounds whip by him, penetrating the space he'd just vacated as he lunged to one side. He hit the magazine release and registered the metal box dropping from the Hi-Power's butt as he launched himself into a shoulder roll to take advantage of the cover offered by the table. Bullets thunked into the wood and ripped splinters into the air. He operated by instinct, slamming the spare clip home and reaching up with his free hand to trip the slide release as he finished his roll and came up on his feet. He didn't bother to aim, just letting the years of experience guide him. He fired six times, tracking the man in a focused assault that jerked the body backward.

The man died on his feet, then fell.

Voight was already streaking for the back door.

"Freeze!" Bolan ordered. "I need you alive, but that doesn't mean all the pieces have to be there."

Voight froze and slowly lifted his arms over his head. "I'm not armed."

Bolan closed the distance between them and took a pair of plastic cuffs from his belt. He cuffed Voight's hands, then seized the plastic restraining strap between them and held his wrists behind his head.

"Are you sure you've got the right guy?" Voight asked. "I don't know you."

"You wouldn't," Bolan said. "And, yeah, I've got the right guy. You're Charley Voight, ex-MI-6 officer and—of late—a broker for assassins. I'm here about the Huntsman and the deal you helped broker regarding the attempt on the prime minister's life."

"I don't know what you're talking about."

"I'm not a cop," the Executioner told him in a graveyard voice. "I can waive your right to a fair and speedy trial by simply putting a bullet in your head."

Voight licked his lips. "Maybe we can deal. I've got money here."

Aware that the numbers were whispering by at an increasing rate of speed, Bolan started the man forward, figuring his personal office was somewhere on the other side of the doorway. "Let's go. I need your personal computer."

Voight went reluctantly but quickly, leading the way through a narrow corridor that branched off in a T. He took the right fork and used a key to open the door on a large office.

The room was immense, occupying a corner space with two windows overlooking the streets. An impressive computer system covered a computer desk set against one wall, butted up against the massive inlaid desk that held only an agenda, a telephone, a cigar humidor and a desk set.

"Bring up the computer," Bolan commanded as he went to the desk and lifted the phone. He kept Voight covered as he dialed the number for Stony Man Farm. Kurtzman answered. "It's Striker. Let me know if he's left anything out." He cradled the phone in the modem and stared into Voight's eyes. "My friends will know if you try to hide anything. Put in your password."

Voight's fingers trembled as he tapped the keys.

"Stand back," Bolan ordered.

The man moved back, his eyes fired with desperation.

With a brief flicker, the monitor suddenly filled with screen after screen of information as Kurtzman's cybernetic vampires sucked the disk drives dry.

"There's a vault in this room," Voight said. "You'll find a button under the edge of the desk. There's a lot of money in there."

Bolan reached under the desk's edge and felt for the button. He was there primarily on a recon mission to find out more about the Huntsman. Time was against him, but he didn't want to leave a stone unturned. The organization the Huntsman had behind him or her or them was obviously massive. When he found the recessed button, he pressed it, not worrying that it might be some kind of alarm. Anyone in the building who didn't know what was going on by now was deaf.

In response to the push, a section of the wall beside the entryway slid to one side. It was dark inside, but lighted well enough that the warrior could see the racks of American and Russian weapons on either side, and rows of currency stacked on shelves at the back of the vault.

"Inside," Bolan said, waving with the gun.

Voight led the way. "You could be a rich man."

The Executioner gave the man a cold look. "With this door open, I could be a rich man whether you lived or died." He riffled the currency, seeing that it was from a number of different countries. Then he noticed the hundred-dollar bills were arranged in stacks that had the same serial numbers. "This is counterfeit."

Voight moved suddenly, ramming his shoulder into the wall beside him. In response, a square fell away in the floor, opening onto a tunnel that had a sudden drop. The mercenary broker rushed toward the opening, but the Executioner was quicker, managing to grab the man's jacket collar and hoist him up. He hauled Voight away from the escape route.

Bolan checked the computer. It was still cycling away. "Where's the Huntsman?"

"I don't know what you're talking about."

Leveling the Browning, Bolan said, "Then you're a dead man."

"Wait." Voight blinked nervously. "I will tell you what I know." He took a deep breath. "The guy is a ghost. But I can get in touch with someone who can put a word in the right ear. A lot of people in my business can."

"Give me a name."

Voight named his contact in Dublin, then gave the address of the bar where the man was known to hang out.

"I don't think the attempt on the prime minister's life is over," Bolan said. "Where can I find the Huntsman?"

"He was here," Voight said. "In the conference room with us when you broke in. He got away."

Bolan knew that explained the open door at the back of the room.

"Now I'm here," a cold, sardonic voice announced.

Stepping back into the shelter of the rifle racks, Bolan glanced out the front of the vault.

A redheaded man with freckles and a scar on his left cheek stood there, holding a Colt .45 Government Model at full extension. "No one betrays the Huntsman," he promised, "and lives." The gun in his hand boomed three times. The .45ACP rounds tore into Voight and bounced him off the vault walls.

Bolan returned fire, but the Huntsman was too quick. The bullets passed through empty air. He went in pursuit at once, proceeding as cautiously as possible, the Browning tight in both hands as he turned around the first doorway. He listened. Above the dulled roar of the air-conditioning, he heard springy steps against carpet heading in the direction of the conference room. He followed without hesitation.

At the doorway to the conference room, he saw the redheaded man stop short. At the opposite doorway, coming in from the maze of offices, were a handful of uniformed London policemen. Some of them had pistols and yelled warnings to the Huntsman to lay down his weapon.

Instead the Huntsman backed away toward the glass wall. "You can't kill me," he snarled. "I'm immortal. I'll rise from my own ashes and strangle you with your own entrails. The Wild Hunt continues." He turned suddenly and emptied the rest of the clip into the glass wall. Without another word, he hurled himself through the weakened glass and plunged to the ground.

Bolan didn't wait around, immediately withdrawing and racing back to Voight's office. He locked the door behind him and checked the computer. The screen was empty. Raising the Browning, he fired it dry, blowing the computer system to bits. An electrical fire started, spewing dark smoke into the air. He paused long enough to grab the phone and smash it to the floor.

He tripped the button under the desk and beat the closing wall. Darkness enveloped him as he felt for the escape route. Remembering the counterfeit money, he reached out for the hundred-dollar bills and stuffed a handful in his pocket. There was no telling where they might lead, but it was another trail left to explore. Then he stepped into the opening.

He dropped and slid like a runaway toboggan, coming to a rough landing on a concrete floor in a different section of darkness. Using a penlight, he located the access switch that opened the wall in front of him, then learned he was in the archives beneath the building. Filing cabinets, bookshelves and banded bundles of yellowed newspapers were everywhere. The dust almost choked him.

It took the warrior less than a minute to find the stairway leading out of the building to street level. Sirens screamed in every direction. Before the arriving London police could properly seal off the block, he'd faded from the area and caught a cab on Chancery Lane, his thoughts already turning to what might be waiting in Dublin.

# EPILOGUE

Dropping money into a pay phone at the Heathrow Airport waiting area, Bolan dialed the Stony Man number. Barbara Price answered. "Me," the warrior said. "Did the Bear get it all?"

"Yes. We still don't know how much it's going to help." In terse sentences that revealed content without useless elaboration, the Stony Man mission controller brought the warrior up to date on everything that had happened with Able Team and Phoenix Force since they'd last spoken.

"We're not working four separate caseloads here," she concluded. "All of these operations tie up. Phoenix turned up a Huntsman working with Bloody Wind in Israel, along with counterfeit money that coincides with counterfeit money Able and Hal recovered at their respective locations."

Bolan reached into his pocket and retrieved the bills he'd taken from Voight's vault. He read off the serial numbers as jet engines screamed overhead. "That ring a bell?"

"Loud and clear. We're tied up all the way around. This thing is bigger than we suspected."

"Explains why all these missions turned priority red all at one time."

Price paused. "We need a sit-down to discuss our next moves."

"I agree." Bolan glanced through the crowd of people filing through the airport. London cops were making the rounds, too, though it didn't necessarily mean they were searching for him. Still, he'd been seen.

"Where?"

"Not here. I need a place I can cool off."

"Name it."

"Dublin. I turned up a lead on the Huntsman that I need to pursue."

"I'll see what's available and get back to you and Jack on the plane."

"Do that." Bolan broke the connection and walked down the hallway to join Grimaldi, waiting at the other end.

"And?" the pilot asked as he fell into step beside the warrior.

"We won the battle but not the war," the Executioner replied. As they walked to their plane, he relayed a thumbnail sketch of the information Price had imparted.

"Well," Grimaldi said, "the way I see it, that puts us one battle up on the opposition."

"It's a start," Bolan agreed. But he knew he was in for the duration. Fighting the savages who were prepared to tear down the civilized world was a quest the Executioner had undertaken. He knew he would eventually give his life in that struggle, and that was acceptable. He'd never flinched from his duty, and he never would.

\* \* \* \* \*

*The heart-stopping action continues in the second book of The Arms Trilogy:* Triburst, *coming in April.*

# Gold Eagle presents a special three-book in-line continuity

THE
ARMS
TRILOGY
★ ★

Beginning in March 1995, Gold Eagle brings you another action-packed three-book in-line continuity, THE ARMS TRILOGY.

In THE ARMS TRILOGY, the men of Stony Man Farm target Hayden Thone, powerful head of an illicit weapons empire. Thone, CEO of Fortress Arms, is orchestrating illegal arms deals and secretly directing the worldwide activities of terrorist groups for his own purposes.

Be sure to catch all the action featuring the ever-popular THE EXECUTIONER starting in March, continuing through to May.

Available at your favorite retail outlet, or order your copy now:

GOLD EAGLE®

AT95-2

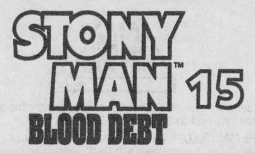

**When all is lost, there is
always the future**

# JAMES AXLER

## DEATH LANDS ®

## Genesis Echo

The warrior survivalists are guests in a reactivated twentieth-
century medical institute in Maine, where mad scientists pursue
their abstract theories, oblivious to the realities of the world. When
they take an unhealthy interest in Krysty Wroth, the pressure is on
to find a way out of this guarded enclave.

In the Deathlands, the war for domination is over, but the struggle
for survival continues.